I0452401

The Glassmaker's Helper

The Getaway Chronicles

DARIE McCOY

Edited By
All That's Wright

Copyright © 2024 by Darie McCoy

All rights reserved.

No part of this book may be reproduced in any form or by any electronic or mechanical means, including information storage and retrieval systems, without written permission from the author, except for the use of brief quotations in a book review.

Edited by: All That's Wright

Cover Art/Design: Royal Touch Photography

Inside Title Page: A.S. McCoy

EBook ISBN: 978-1-961999-09-1

Print ISBN: 978-1-961999-94-7

For everyone with big ideas. Keep dreaming. Keep trying.

Contents

Prologue

"One will come, and she will wield magicks which haven't been seen in this realm for generations. She will be born to the blood of Leander. Through her, the line will be restored."

The words the old enchantress had spoken all those revolutions ago played on a loop in Ophelia's head. While the white-haired elder had the ability to work roots, and other natural substances to promote healing, her primary blessing, the one revealed to her during her visit to the Glassmaker as a youngling, was precognition. With a touch, the enchantress could predict a being's future.

Her gift wasn't to be conjured upon demand. One couldn't come to her with the expectation that she would tell a fortune like the carnival acts of other realms. No, the enchantress would be given a vision, and send for the person for whom it was meant. It was custom to reward her with a gift upon receiving the fruit of her blessing.

A blessing which had never steered a soul wrong. At least not until she'd spoken those words to Ophelia's great-grandmother while she carried Ophelia's grandfather in her womb. Three generations later, Ophelia was the first and only female born in the Leander line. From the moment of her birth, there was the expectation she would be the salvation of their family.

At the age of five, the youngest age a youngling could be presented to the Glassmaker, Ophelia stood before the large male who wore a worn leather apron. Before them, were shards of glass inside wooden bowls in varying shades. The man's dark, sharp eyes stared at her from his great height making her want to shrink behind her father's leg, but she remained where she was—waiting for the process she'd watched a few times by that point in her life.

What should've happened was the Glassmaker selecting from the array of colored pieces, then shaping and molding them into a form. The form wasn't the important part of the process. No. It was the sparks that flew while he worked the piece. The bright flashes were the tea leaves he read to discern the blessing of the individual who'd been presented to him.

Instead of the process going as it should have, the Glassmaker stared at Ophelia with a dull expression. His large arms were folded across his chest, and he made no move to grab any of the tools he'd need to begin the task.

"Is there a problem, Glassmaker?"

Theron Leander, Ophelia's father, placed one hand on Ophelia's shoulder. His large palm offered her comfort as her little body had begun to tremble with nervousness the longer it took the Glassmaker to begin.

"I have no blessing for this youngling."

Gasps and murmurs came from the crowd gathered in the semi-circle around the large man's work area. The heat from the fire he used to melt the glass should've warded off the cold, but a chill washed over Ophelia with his words. Her small arms wrapped themselves around her torso as far as she could reach in an attempt to ward it off.

"That's impossible. The enchantress said my daughter would have a powerful blessing."

"I can't speak on what the enchantress has foreseen, but I have no blessing for *this* youngling. Perhaps the enchantress was wrong."

The murmurs grew louder when he said those last words. *Wrong?* The enchantress was never wrong. She was gifted with extended life because of the way her blessing had guided the people in their realm to flourish. To even imply that her vision wasn't accurate was tantamount to blasphemy.

"The enchantress is *never* wrong. Perhaps *your* blessing is failing *you*."

Ophelia had never heard such fierceness in her father's voice. He was normally slow to anger. But when she looked up into his face, his brows were lowered darkly above his amber eyes which stood out in contrast against his dark brown skin. The Glassmaker unfolded his arms, letting them hang at his sides with his fingers bent to make fists.

Added warmth landed on Ophelia's other shoulder and she turned to see her mother. She had one hand on Ophelia, and the other on her husband and life mate.

"Glassmaker, we mean no disrespect. Is it possible for you to work the glass anyway? Maybe her blessing won't be clear until the glass is shaped."

As a youngling, Ophelia didn't have full comprehension of the tension in the moment, but she recalled the sense of relief she felt when the Glassmaker yielded to her mother's request. The respite was short lived. When he reached the point in the process where he was to shape the glass at the end of his long metal tool, instead of the sparks which normally shot out from the piece, the glass shattered. It returned to the shards he'd scooped from the wooden bowls lined up on the workman's bench.

The silence which followed was louder than any of the murmurs that had blazed through the crowd previously. Her mother's cries finally pierced the quiet. The sound had haunted Ophelia since that moment. It was a shadow which loomed each time they went to a new place to find a different Glassmaker, one with a stronger blessing than the others. One who could finally confirm the future foreseen by the enchantress.

It had been almost thirty winters since the first time her parents had taken her before the Glassmaker. The passing time had been difficult for her family. They still worked hard, using their blessings to bring honor to their line, but she felt the weight of the unfulfilled prophecy with each passing season.

When her older brother, Damien stopped his horse, her steed heeded the unspoken command, bringing her up alongside him. Eyes filled with fatigue met hers.

"This is the last one, Phely. There are no others we can seek out. If he turns us away…"

Damien didn't have to say anything more. Ophelia heard the words unspoken. If this Glassmaker couldn't discern her gift, they'd have to concede that the enchantress was indeed wrong in her prediction.

Chapter One

Rylan felt them before he saw them. The group of strangers who had come to his workshop on the outskirts of the village. Unlike the Glassmakers before him, he didn't relish the attention garnered from being the discerner of blessings. So, he didn't make a home at the village hub so that each time he delivered a blessing, he could be assured a crowd of spectators.

He believed learning of one's blessing, their gift which they would use to aid or advance their people in some way, was a personal experience. The most he allowed to attend were close family members and a Chronicler. The latter was a necessity as they were required to record such things.

Each village had one, but each Chronicler supplied records to the Keeper. They in turn wrote of the blessings in The Ledger. It held the history of the people in the realm from the time of the written word. It was rumored to contain the accountings from the very beginning of their kind.

Opening the heavy metal door, Rylan stepped out onto the top stair. Sitting atop their mounts were the strangers he'd sensed from inside. Their steeds were fit, coats reflecting the obvious attention paid to their grooming and care.

Saying nothing, Rylan stood with his arms folded across his chest. A large, barrel-chested male wearing the simple clothing of a Seeker dismounted and approached him.

"Glassmaker?" The man's tentative question belied the sureness of his approach. With each step made, he placed his foot with purpose.

"Yes. Who is asking?"

"I am Damien of the Leander. I've come on behalf of my family."

Nodding, Rylan slightly relaxed his stance, but remained watchful. This Damien hadn't yet said why he'd come, only who he represented. Three other males sat on mounts in front of a fourth, who was obscured from Rylan's view.

"We seek your reading of the glass for my sister."

Rylan looked at the other man's attire consisting of dark close-fitting trousers with multiple pockets and a shirt with sleeves covering his arms down to his wrists. A leather strap bisected his chest with a quiver of arrows attached. The corresponding bow was affixed to the saddle of his horse.

"You're not from the village." It was a statement, but the Leander took it for what it was, a request for information.

"No. We're from the valley. We traveled for seven rotations to get here."

"Do you not have a Glassmaker in the valley?"

"We do."

"Why did you not take your sister there?"

"We did. Many revolutions ago. He was unable to name her blessing."

Rylan's eyes narrowed. Parents didn't typically take their youngling to the Glassmaker unless some sort of ability had already been witnessed. Not everyone was among the blessed. So, those who hadn't detected anything beyond the normal abilities didn't waste the Glassmaker's time. He'd only heard of once where a Glassmaker was unable to name a youngling's blessing.

It was nearly thirty winters ago by one of his father's brothers. Was it possible the Leander was requesting a blessing for an adult? If a blessing doesn't manifest before a person reached seventeen winters, then they were deemed unblessed. There was no shame in it.

Sure, the blessed were praised in some circles, but those without distinct blessings were still able to make valuable contributions. Younglings were malleable. Once their blessing was determined, they were taught to maximize it and use it in a way that promoted growth amongst their people—not harm. Adults weren't as easily trained. They had a lifetime of experiences which bred insecurities, and fears as easily as over-confidence in their ability to quickly master a skill.

Rylan stared at the assembled men. An unknown feeling had been pulsing beneath his skin from the moment he sensed the strangers' presence. Rylan couldn't place it. Despite his reservations, instinct compelled him to grant the Leander's request.

"Bring her to me."

Not waiting for a response, he turned on his heel and went back inside his workshop. Walking to his furnace he checked to make certain the fire still blazed hot enough to keep the glass inside liquid. In a practiced routine, he set out the bowls containing the multi-colored frit he'd combine with the liquid glass. When he twisted to retrieve a rod from the collection mounted on one wall, he nearly stumbled at the vision framed in the doorway.

"Hello, Glassmaker. Thank you for agreeing to see me."

The vision's voice skated over his skin leaving goosebumps in its wake. Unbidden, Rylan's gaze roved over her form appreci-ating the breeches she wore beneath the long, loose fitting ladies' top cinched at the waist by a wide belt. The accessory accentuated the dip of her waist above the flaring of her rounded hips. Her full lips begged for his kisses. Prominent cheekbones kept her face from being completely round, making for a beauty worthy of stealing his breath. All the moisture left his mouth, and Rylan wasn't certain he remembered how to form words.

A jerky nod was all he managed before quickly turning away without grabbing the rod. Keeping busy adding more frit to the assembled bowls, he coached himself to contain the uncharacteristic feelings. He was behaving like a lad who'd yet to have his first rut. Drawing on the control he'd mastered as an apprentice, he was finally able to go back to get the rod he'd forgotten. Not looking directly at the beautiful creature, he pointed to the bowls.

"Come this way."

His voice sounded gruff to his own ears, but it couldn't be helped. His movements were totally from muscle memory. All of his concentration was required for that. Modulating his voice wasn't a part of the deal.

An enticing scent tickled his nose just as the tips of her booted feet entered his line of sight as he fixed his stare on the frit. Refraining from breathing deeply, he lifted his gaze again. She was just as beautiful up close, and infinitely more alluring. But her loveliness wasn't what made him forget to release his breath.

Shades of purple, and lavender with streaks of white appeared to outline her form. It was unlike anything he'd ever seen in his many winters as a Glassmaker. Without tearing his gaze away, he rearranged the bowls, stacking them until two remained between them. Only then did he go to the crucible to gather the clear glass onto the end of the rod.

The transparent base had no magical properties on its own. Neither did the frit which appeared to be tiny shards of glass to the unknowing eye. The magick flowed through the

Glassmaker themselves. The glass was simply the conduit through which their blessing manifested. The energy pulsing around them, when he dipped the glass into each vessel to pick up individual colors of frit, made the hair at his nape stand on end.

At that stage, Rylan felt himself fall into a trance-like state. The heat from the furnace kept the room warm to the point of sweating, but he felt nothing as he turned the glass to blend the colors into the translucent, nor when he stretched and twisted it like a candy maker working taffy. He didn't fully come to himself until he began shaping. When the coolness of the wood block touched the hot glass, sparks matching the colorful aura surrounding the Leander beauty, flew from the glass.

Only revolutions of experience kept him from dropping his tools and ending the process. The pulsing he'd felt earlier increased to such proportions he thought his heart would escape his chest. *It couldn't be. Such a blessing hadn't been bestowed in over a thousand revolutions.*

Yet, the sparks had never lied to him. Fighting the trembling in his digits, he continued to shape the piece to completion. When he was done, the shades of purple and white appeared to swirl inside the clear glass. It was as if a whirling wind had been painted in those colors and captured inside a globe, which fit in the palm of his hand.

Using cooling leathers, he placed it inside the cabinet he used to allow his creations to set. When he turned back toward the others, five sets of identical amber eyes stared at him expectantly. Rylan shucked off his protective gear tossing it onto the workbench. Their anticipation was palpable, but the magnitude of what he had to reveal to them kept him silent longer than usual.

"Please. Please just tell me. This isn't my first time. It will simply be the last. If it is meant for me to concede, I'd rather know the answer. That way I can move on from this precarious existence I've lived up to this point."

The near brokenness of her spirit reached out and grabbed Rylan's heart, squeezing it until he didn't think it would continue to function as it should. He couldn't imagine the life she'd lived. Although he hadn't said so aloud, he'd concluded she was the same female who'd been denied a blessing all those revolutions ago.

If he'd heard of what she'd gone through with the first Glassmaker, it was no doubt everyone in the area she lived was aware. How they must have regarded at her with pitying stares each time they passed her. He couldn't allow his tongue to be still a moment longer.

"The sparks... Your blessing... You are Ergokin."

Her thick lashes lifted, revealing green flecks in her amber eyes. Her stunned expression mirrored his feelings on the matter. Although hers had more than a tinge of the disbelief he experienced when the blessing was revealed. The way she searched his face, he knew she was trying to find any deception on his part. She wouldn't find any. There was a slight tremble in her fingers which were twisted together in front of her. One of her kin broke the nonverbal standoff.

"There hasn't been a recording of Ergokin in more than a millennia. How is that possible?"

Rylan regarded him with his normal implacable continence. "I'm the Glassmaker. Not a Seer nor a Diviner. I can only say what is revealed to me through the sparks. The rest is not my domain."

Looking at the beauty, he realized he didn't know her name. He knew none of their names, with the exception of the first. Damien of the Leander. Based on their resemblance to one another, he'd deemed them family. Not being able to name the other three males didn't bother him, but not knowing the creator-given name of the beauty did.

He'd barely restrained himself from calling her sweeting, when he told her of her blessing. Unmated and never interested in tying himself to another body, Rylan couldn't explain the compulsion to give her pretty words, calm her fears, and remove anything which might cause her even the slightest discomfort.

Heat blazed beneath his skin when she laid a soft hand on his forearm. She attempted to snatch it back almost immediately, but he captured her digits holding them in place.

"My apologies. I didn't mean to be so forward, Glassmaker."

"Rylan. You may call me Rylan. And it's okay."

Long lashes hid her eyes from him briefly, before she looked up at him again.

"I am called Ophelia." A shy smile hovered at the corners of her full lips, but Rylan detected her nervousness beneath the gesture. Clearing her throat, she spoke again.

"Rylan, please forgive us. But I've been presented to Glassmakers all over the realm since I was a youngling. I don't discount your discernment, but Ergokin are considered a myth. A legend that no one in living memory can say they've encountered."

Without conscious thought, his thumb stroked the back of her hand. The silkiness of it would've been completely distracting if he hadn't felt the racing of her pulse. Attributing it to her distress, he sought a way to soothe her. He took no offense to her statement. Even knowing that had it been anyone other than her, he would've been tempted to snap their neck at a hint they didn't believe his declaration.

"She's right. Besides, our family has Seekers, Changers, Earthers, and a few Vanes. There isn't one Ergokin in the Leander line."

Not taking his gaze from Ophelia's, Rylan kept his focus

on her. She nodded in agreement with Damien, but hoped glimmered deep within those jeweled eyes.

"No matter of how long it has been or how the others in your line were blessed... *The sparks don't lie*. You are Ergokin."

He could tell she wanted to believe him. Her fingers flexed against his forearm like she was gripping the line tethering her to life. Something inside him wanted desperately to be that tether. So much so, that his mouth spoke without consulting his brain.

"I can take you to the Keeper. I have never met an Ergokin before. So, I don't know of a being who can help you master your gift. But there should be something written in the Ledger."

Chapter Two

Ophelia stared up into the rugged, square jawed face of the Glassmaker—Rylan. He didn't have the soft handsomeness which bordered on pretty that she'd seen on the males in and around her village. His prominent nose was proud. Thick lashes and almost bushy eyebrows shielded his dark green eyes making them look nearly black. The open neck of his tunic revealed a sliver of dark markings on his skin.

Gazing upon him had an unfamiliar effect on her. Because of her lack of experience with the feeling, she didn't know how to categorize it. She just knew something about him called to her—more than just her desire for him to be the conduit for her blessing to be told.

His height and bulkiness had initially reminded her of the Glassmaker she'd been presented to as a youngling. His gruff voice did as well. However, once she was able to see past those things, she realized he was nothing like the Glassmaker from all those revolutions ago. Such a male would never have agreed to read the sparks for someone who'd seen as many winters as she had.

Ophelia still didn't understand how the other male had

deemed her unblessed without even attempting to work the glass. Every other her family had taken her to, had at least done that much before the shattered glass confirmed the edict of the first. Each of those previous times, her anxiety had been so heightened, she'd tried to will the sparks to appear. Sometimes, the Glassmaker made it to the shaping before the glass shattered. But, oftentimes, the results were the same as with the first Glassmaker.

When Rylan volunteered to take her to the Keeper, Ophelia's breath caught in her throat. No one got an audience with the Keeper. Only the Chroniclers and the Keeper's closest attendants ever saw her. However, Glassmakers were the only beings who could discern the blessings of others—even future Keepers. So, if there was one among them who could gain an audience with her, it would be him.

"You would do that? Take me to the Keeper?"

The slight roughness of the pad of his thumb reminded her of the hand he clamped over hers on his forearm. The contact was simultaneously comforting and...something else...

"Of course, Sweeting."

An unfamiliar tingle fluttered in Ophelia's belly with the endearment. The trace of softness in his eyes captured her attention to the point she nearly forgot what he was agreeing to. Clanging taps to the door broke the spell weaving between them.

Ophelia looked over her shoulder to see her brothers all turn with their hands at their hips ready to draw their weapons if necessary. Before she could glimpse who their protective stance was aimed at, Rylan had tucked her behind his wide frame.

"Glassmaker!" A male voice boomed into the space. "There you are!"

Ophelia peeked around Rylan to see a male draped in finery. He was obviously of the upper class of this village—

possibly the whole realm from the jewels adorning his fingers. A fur lined cape was clasped on one side by an intricately curved piece of fine metal, leaving one shoulder uncovered.

She wondered why he felt it necessary to speak as if he'd been searching for Rylan without success. It was easy enough for Damien to get the location of his workshop from an elderly couple in the village. His location wasn't hidden by any means. The male's presence was so overbearing, she nearly missed the little boy standing slightly behind him on his left.

"Caspian."

Rylan didn't sound as if he welcomed a visit from this, Caspian. In fact, he hooked an arm around her gently pressing her behind him again, interrupting her perusal of the situation. Part of her wanted to stamp her foot in protest. But, being raised by a protective father in the presence of four brothers who followed in his footsteps, Ophelia recognized a losing battle when she saw one.

"I told you I would seek you out when Sebastian was older. He's seven winters now. I've come for you to give us his blessing."

With her only view that of Rylan's back, Ophelia didn't miss the tightening across his shoulders. His dark brown hair was swept up atop his head, tied by a leather string into a messy knot. So, it was easy for her to see the stiffness in his back extending up to his neck. Whatever the reason, the finely dressed male put Rylan on alert.

However, despite his obvious distrust in his new visitor, Rylan didn't ignore the request hidden behind the declaration. His large hand appeared behind his back. Instinctively, she placed her palm in his. The heat of his protection flowed through the digits closed around hers as he guided her to the side of the room farthest away from the new arrival, and nearest her brother, Jaime. During the short trek, he kept himself between her and the new arrivals. She couldn't see them and it was unlikely they could see her. After Rylan positioned her behind her largest brother, an unspoken conversation occurred between the two before Rylan walked away.

Ophelia was shocked at the liberties her brothers were allowing the Glassmaker to take. They normally ran suitors off in a hail of arrows—literally. Yet, they'd said nothing as Rylan had appointed himself her primary protector. She watched the sureness of his gait, confounded by the turn of events.

"Come." Rylan said, as he gestured to the boy.

Peeking around Jaime, Ophelia watched him. The gruffness in his voice was slightly tempered from when he'd spoke to Caspian. Ophelia concluded his normal speech tended toward brusque rather than soft spoken. The revelation was oddly comforting.

While his steps were tentative, the copper haired boy followed Rylan's command, only stopping when he was within arm's reach of the workbench. Donning his protective garments, Rylan stared at him. The widening of the Glassmaker's eyes was so slight, had she not been watching him so intently, Ophelia would've missed it. It was as if he was taken aback by what he saw when he looked at the boy.

"What's your name?"

"I told you, this is—"

"I was speaking to the boy." Rylan cut off Caspian's attempt to speak for the youngling.

"Sebastian." In a clear, high voice, the boy responded.

Caspian's audible huff wasn't acknowledged by anyone, least of all Rylan. Who, with a curt nod, began arranging the bowls of colored glass on the table similarly to the way he'd done when he was preparing to read the sparks for Ophelia.

Now that the pressure of her own reading was off her shoulders, Ophelia watched Rylan work. She was mesmerized by the confidence in his movements as he selected the different colored glass shards. Where he'd use two bowls for her, he

selected three for Sebastian. As before, no one spoke while
Rylan worked.

From what Ophelia could determine, the rest of them
ceased to exist while the Glassmaker went about his tasks. The
protective leather covering his extremities didn't hide his
bulging muscles, which contracted and relaxed during the
process of heating, twisting, and working the hot substance.
During the shaping, the sparks shooting from beneath the
wood shaper were bright blue, green and aqua.

Due to her many visits with Glassmakers and revolutions
of watching others receive their blessings, Ophelia recognized
the combination. The little boy was likely Hydrokin. It was a
type of elemental who could control water. They were as vital
as Vanes in farming villages as they could manipulate the moisture in the very air to supply rain to crops. She'd even heard of
Hydrokin who could change the flow of rivers and streams—
very powerful beings.

When Rylan was done, the piece before him was a beautiful wide-mouthed vessel. The pattern of the colors resembled
tumultuous ocean waves. Ophelia was in awe. Not simply of
Rylan's ability to use glass to reveal a being's blessing, but in
his skill with the substance. Watching him open the large
cabinet to place the piece inside, she saw other stunning
creations lining the shelves. She wondered what it was like to
be able to fashion such beauty with one's own hands.

Rylan had barely turned away after closing the doors of
the cabinet before Caspian was prompting him.

"Well?"

Ignoring him again, Rylan removed his protective apron
and sleeves, as he returned to stand in front of Sebastian.
Lowering himself until he was eye-level with the boy, he stared
at him for a second before speaking.

"Sebastian, you are blessed with Hydrokin. Do you know
what that means?"

Sebastian nodded mutely. His wide eyes reflecting the colors of the piece now hidden inside Rylan's cabinet.

"Good." Giving Sebastian's slim shoulder two quick taps, Rylan stood to his full height. It was then he gave Caspian his attention.

"He will need to see the Chronicler. They'll help find him a mentor to teach him to control and master his blessing."

Caspian's pale face was tinged with red. He appeared as if he wanted to say or do awful things to Rylan. While Ophelia had no knowledge of their prior relationship, the way Caspian carried himself said he was a male accustomed to being treated a certain way. The manner in which Rylan responded to him was possibly shocking in the lack of respect given his obvious station.

However, no matter the harsh words he likely wanted to say, he didn't voice them. Instead, he reached beneath the cape and produced a pouch. The contents clanged in a way known to Ophelia as he dropped it on the workbench atop one of Rylan's leather sleeves. His thin lips were stretched even thinner as he placed a hand on Sebastian's shoulder pulling the boy away from Rylan.

"Good rotation, Glassmaker. Thank you for your service."

Somehow, Ophelia didn't think Caspian was thankful for the blessing Rylan proclaimed. Being Hydrokin probably didn't appeal to a being who obviously valued wealth and station. The Hydrokin Ophelia knew of had usually worked in tandem with Earthers in various forms of farming. Caspian didn't have the air of a farmer.

Scooping up the pouch, Rylan didn't bother to look inside. Instead, he walked to the door, closing it and latching it behind his uninvited guests. His action tickled her memory of when the two arrived. She didn't recall them opening the door. By the time she'd seen them, they were standing in the open doorway. Rylan confirmed her suspicions when he came back to her. Taking her hand in his, he waved the other at her brothers.

"Come with me. I don't know how much he heard before he decided to let us know he was there."

Looking from Rylan's rigid profile to her brothers, Ophelia tried to catch up with the implications of his statement. Caspian didn't strike her as one who cared about anything beyond what personally affected him. So, she didn't completely understand Rylan's change in demeanor.

She only caught glimpses of the interior of his home as Rylan led them down a long corridor ending in a round room with two additional hallways on the other side of the cozy space, leading away from it. She hadn't been able to so much as peek into the rooms with open doors as they passed. All of her attention was on keeping up with his long strides. Although she was taller than many males she'd met, Rylan had at least three hands on Ophelia's height.

Once they were all in the room, Rylan released her hand. Her gaze swept around the area. While sparsely furnished, it still held a warmth about it. There was a hearth taking up a large portion of one wall. A large black pot, similar to a sorcerer's cauldron hung from a hook over the flame.

"When was the last time you rested your mounts? Are they fresh enough to ride until dark?"

Ophelia whirled from the fire to stare at Rylan. He was addressing her brother Damien who didn't seem to consider the question strange.

"What's going on, Rylan? Why do we need to leave?"

Chapter Three

Under Ophelia's probing stare, Rylan appeared to be trying to put some space between them. She couldn't discern why, but his actions implied he wanted to hide her away. However, when she said his name, he came right back to her side.

Observing him closely, she allowed him to guide her to sit on the long couch. He glanced at her brothers indicating they should do the same.

"Sweeting, I suspect Caspian overheard me telling you of your blessing."

"Okay, but why is that a problem? It isn't uncommon for those outside of the Glassmaker and family to hear the announcement of a blessing."

"True." Rylan rubbed his fingers across the backs of her hands. Ophelia wasn't sure if it was to soothe her or himself.

"I know it happens, but Caspian Ironshade is a greedy manipulator, and I'm not simply talking about his ability to reshape metals. I'm talking about his desire to use his blessing and the ones of those around him to build an empire he controls.

He can't be trusted with the information that there is a

living Ergokin within the realm. If the goddess revoked blessings, I'd submit Caspian's name to be the first to receive the honor."

"You're saying our sister is in danger."

Damien's statement made the situation abundantly clear to Ophelia. She'd spent her life with the prophecy from the Enchantress hanging over her head, and her family's expectation that her blessing would be what restored honor and reverence to the Leander line. It had always seemed unfair to her. Not because of the hopes placed in her, but because it ignored the contributions of all the others born before and after her.

The Leander family had almost as many blessed as unblessed. Why were the efforts of those members not enough to do those things? No one had ever even told her how the family had lost honor to begin with. Yet, her birth and the blessing she received was supposed to herald a restoration of the Leander line?

"Instinct tells me, yes. If Caspian, or those like him, think they can gain access to the power an Ergokin is rumored to possess through your sister, they will try to take her. In order to prevent that, we need to leave. Going to the Keeper is now more important than ever. We won't register anything with the Chronicler for now. The wind could carry their recording to the wrong ears too quickly."

Standing, her brother Jaime walked toward the corridor they'd previously taken.

"I'll get the horses ready. Kieran, with me."

As the second oldest, Jaime was accustomed to anticipating Damien's instructions. The only Brawn in their generation, he was blessed with extraordinary strength. So, he also considered himself their chief protector.

Without thinking, Ophelia turned her hands beneath Rylan's entwining their digits together. Squeezing them, she tried to draw strength from the confidence he exuded.

"That male...Caspian...and other males think they can just take a being and use them however they see fit?"

Her sheltered existence made the prospect unfathomable to Ophelia. Being whispered about for her parent's refusal to accept her as unblessed? Having no suitors and being unmated well beyond the age of most, both male and female? Those things she understood. Yet, what Rylan suggested confounded her.

However, she'd also been wary of the finely dressed malethe moment he made his presence known in the doorway. With the newly acquired information from Rylan, she now wondered about the boy in his care. Was Sebastian his offspring or another who'd be used for what treasure could be obtained from the use of his gift?

And...since Caspian hadn't appeared to be impressed with the blessing of Hydrokin, would Sebastian suffer because his ability wasn't spectacular enough? Ophelia's mind whirled with thoughts and concerns for herself and the youngling. She was frozen, unsure of how she was to navigate this new dynamic.

Rylan placed his large palm on the side of her face, cupping her cheek with slightly roughened warmth. Instinctively, she leaned into it.

"Sweeting, I know this is unexpected. But, we mustn't dally. Go with your brothers, I'll be there shortly."

Why did his touch offer her such comfort? Why were his words the ones offering her the most reassurance? Ophelia had no answers and no time to delve into the reasons for her automatic acceptance and trust in him. Nodding, she stood when he tugged gently at her fingers.

Amazingly enough, neither of her brothers said anything until they were standing near their mounts. Jaime and Kieran had already brought them closer to the workshop after removing their feeding bags. Ophelia rubbed her hand along her mount's flank. The wetness of Starlight's muzzle said her brothers had watered them as well.

"Now that we're alone, can you tell the rest of us why we are letting the Glassmaker touch our sister like she belongs to him?"

Ramo stared at Damien while gathering the reins of his mount from Kieran. Being directly in the middle of their sibling group, he tended to keep his own counsel most times. So, the question must have been burning his mind for him to give it voice.

Instead of answering, Damien glanced at Ophelia, then back to Ramo. "We'll discuss it later."

Normally, that would be the end of it. Despite their number of winters, they all yielded to their father as their patriarch. When he wasn't present, as the eldest, Damien assumed the role. It was so rare for any of them to question him every jaw dropped when Ophelia spoke up.

"Why must he wait for later to discuss it, Damien? Is it because you don't want me to know?" With Starlight's reigns fisted in one hand, she stared at him.

"It's not for you to know, Phely."

Dropping the reigns, she stalked over to him. Angry heat licked up her cheeks as she stood before him.

"It's not for me to know? How is that possible, Damien, when *I'm* the one being discussed? Why wouldn't I need to know about things involving me? I'm well past being a youngling's age. I don't require coddling."

"Phely..." Kieran's voice had a combination of pleading and warning in its quality, but Ophelia held up a hand warding him off.

"No, Kieran. We've followed Damien without question from the moment the sun kissed our skin. And that's fine, but I won't be dismissed as if things dealing with me directly shouldn't be spoken about in *my* presence. That will not stand."

Seeming to feel her rising ire, Starlight danced closer, nuzzling Ophelia's arm. Absently rubbing the beast between the ears, she stared at her eldest brother with a fierce expression. She refused to back down. Eventually, Damien realized she had no intention of letting it go.

"He's your mate."

The air whooshed from Ophelia's lungs. A brush from a feather quill could have toppled her onto her backside at that moment. After an indeterminant length of time, she was finally able to close her mouth again—blinking slowly as she continued to regard her brother in disbelief.

"He's my *what*?"

Once her faculties began to function again, her heart raced as if it was trying to gallop right out of her chest. Placing one hand above her breast, she pressed her palm there as if it would keep the unruly organ in place. It wasn't possible. Her ears weren't working properly. Damien hadn't said the Glassmaker was her mate. She resigned herself to living out her revolutions unmated.

Being the doting aunt, and helping with her siblings' younglings was what she imagined for her future. Not being mated and definitely not to a Glassmaker. He must be mistaken. Dashing her hopes that Damien was wrong, Kieran spoke up again.

"He *is* your mate, Phely."

Ophelia could doubt Damien; he was a Seeker. He could find anyone and anything that was lost or needed finding. Recognizing the thread tying two beings together wasn't an ability he possessed. But, it *was* the blessing bestowed on Kieran. From the time he was six winters old, he'd been able to see the cord binding two souls together. What was invisible to everyone else, shone brightly to him.

Turning toward him, Ophelia stared into his eyes seeing the truth written there. When had he known? When had he had a chance to say something to Damien and the others? The knowledge explained her unquestioned trust of the Glassmaker. However, it was also terrifying.

Chapter Four

Once the siblings walked out of his common room, Rylan made haste to pack a satchel with the items he considered most critical to him on a journey. Recalling that they'd arrived without a large store of provisions, he realized he'd need to take his wagon and additional supplies.

When he passed through his workshop, he retrieved the wooden box with the travel version of his Glassmaker tools. He also wrapped the small, rounded globe he'd created after reading the sparks for Ophelia.

It was still hot, so he took care to place it in a small box. Constructed similarly to the kiln he used to cool his pieces, it was designed to safely house glass creations that hadn't gone through the cooling process completely. When he'd made the container, he had no idea the circumstances under which he'd be forced to use it.

Many who came to him returned later to retrieve the visual representation of their blessing, but not all did. However, he hadn't had a being travel over a great distance for his services. There were dozens of Glassmakers throughout the realm. It was unnecessary to specifically seek him out.

It took him longer than he would've liked, but he finally drove around the corner of the workshop to see the siblings lined up in front waiting on their mounts.

"We thought we were going to have to leave without you, Glassmaker."

Ophelia's largest brother spoke when Rylan stopped next to them. Not responding to him, Rylan looked to his sweeting. She was seated on a large mare with a shiny mahogany coat. The steed's long black mane was braided with silver ropes threaded through. The silver matched the trim on the cape now resting around Ophelia's shoulders.

Capturing her gaze, Rylan motioned to the tufted seat next to him in the wagon.

"You've ridden a long way, Sweeting. Perhaps you should ride with me or lay down in the back to have a rest."

Rylan had placed bedding inside the covered portion of the wagon anticipating Ophelia's need.

"No, thank you."

Her chin lifted and her posture was straight when she responded. Something had changed in the short time they'd been separated. However, he didn't press the issue. Making a clicking noise in his throat, he flicked the reigns to get Thunderhoof moving toward the road leading away from his home.

"Leander, before we see the Keeper, we should go to your home village."

"Do you think that's wise? Won't it be leading Caspian directly to the place he'd be certain to find Phely? Not to mention others he may covet."

Rylan nodded. He'd considered it, but he also considered the strength of increasing their numbers. Caspian had some power, but even he couldn't raise a force formidable enough to raze an entire village in such a short amount of time.

"Is your family large, and do they have alliances with others?"

"Of course."

The Leander looked offended that Rylan would even suggest they wouldn't have others who'd stand shoulder to shoulder with them if necessary.

"Good. It would be best for your sister's protection to alert them of the possible threat before we seek the counsel of the Keeper."

Following Rylan's explanation, Damien nodded and moved his horse to the front to lead their group away. The biggest brother guided his horse to the back of the wagon where Rylan had tethered his mount, Shadowfox. Once everyone was in position with Ophelia riding at the center, they set off at an easy pace. Rylan wanted to go faster, but knew they had a decent head start on whomever Caspian may send to scout his workshop or the roads.

They made it to their first stop when it became too dark to safely travel. While all of the Leanders were blessed, none was a Luminary. So, they had no choice but to make camp. Damien found a water source. He and Ramo took the horses to drink, and to collect some for the group as well.

Although he didn't ask them, they took Rylan's horses with them. Ophelia busied herself gathering wood to make a fire. The nights could get cool, but since there was the possibility they were being followed, it might not be the best idea. However, he sensed she needed an activity to keep her busy. They didn't talk much on the journey or before. So, he was certain she was still attempting to understand everything happening to and around her.

Keeping his guard up, Rylan prepared the inside of the wagon. He was certain she would object to the arrangement, but he fixed the bedding in anticipation of her sleeping inside. The rest of the brothers were either putting out bed rolls or scouting while staying within sight of Ophelia. It was obvious that they were protective of her.

Rylan had no siblings. So, he couldn't relate to their fraternal bond, but it pleased him to know his Sweeting had such loyal protectors.

"Sweeting, I don't think we can have a fire tonight."

Ophelia stood with a small stack of dry twigs and short branches. There was already a pile at the center of the stones she'd found. Seeing how far along she was in the process, Rylan felt a twinge of guilt for letting it get so far. When her face scrunched and her brow furrowed, he hurried to explain.

"We can't risk the smoke being seen. Even with the measures your brothers took to obscure our trail, it's likely that Caspian's males are looking for any trace of where you've gone."

Even though the brothers revealed they weren't a part of a regular protection force or mercenaries, they were skilled in areas beyond the abilities they were blessed with. As such, Rylan was impressed at the measures they took to throw any potential trackers off their trail.

Rylan watched as Ophelia visibly processed what he said. Then, she stooped down, placing the remaining wood onto the pile. After they were arranged, she stood and brushed her hands down the front of her clothing. He'd been aware of her feminine curves from the moment she stepped into his workshop. However, her movements drew his attention to her abundant bosom and rounded hips.

When her gaze snapped to his, he turned towards his wagon. Considering the way she'd baulked at joining him earlier, he was certain she wouldn't accept the more comfortable sleeping environment. So, he pulled out the items he'd brought for her comfort along with food rations. Once he was certain of where she planned to bed down for the night, he arranged the blankets and pillows placing the food pouch nearby.

"What are you doing, Glassmaker?" Her melodic voice held a tinge of censure.

"Rylan, Sweeting. Call me Rylan."

Crouched as he was positioning the bedding, he had to look up to connect their eyes. While her words said one thing, the softness he saw there, said something different. She was not immune to him either.

"What are you doing, Rylan?"

"I'm preparing a place for you to sleep comfortably. Since we cannot have a fire, I brought you extra blankets to keep you warm in the cool night air."

"You aren't going to volunteer to share your body heat with me?"

"Would you accept it?" Rylan would gladly offer himself as her personal pillow and body warmer, but he didn't see it as an option available to him at the moment.

"No. Other than your craft, I don't know you."

"Then let us rectify that. Come, sit and we can talk."

Extending his hand, Rylan waited for her to accept his assistance getting comfortable on the nest he'd constructed for her. She studied him for a moment before slipping her hand into his. His eyes nearly closed from the pleasure of feeling her soft palm glide across his.

Once she was seated, he passed her the pouch containing the food. Then, he sat on his own bedroll he'd placed nearby.

"Is that where you plan to sleep?" Ophelia gestured to his proximity to her sleeping mat.

The innocent wariness in her expression brought a smile to his face. Her question confirmed his suspicion. She had no experience with the carnal side of relations between a male and a female. But, she was versed enough to be cautious. Although, he'd have to be exceedingly brave or foolish to believe her brothers would tolerate him attempting to share mats with their only sister.

"No, Sweeting. I will be nearby, but not this close." Rylan indicated his mats a few feet away. "I'll be just over there when it is time for me to rest for the night. Now, I wanted to be able to speak to you without raised voices."

"Oh." Ophelia folded her hands on her lap atop the pouch he'd given her. She hadn't even loosened the laces to see what was inside.

Since they were trying to put as much distance between themselves and possible pursuers, they hadn't stopped long enough to eat a meal. Although he thought she should eat something, Rylan didn't press. Instead, he watched Ophelia, feeling the unease wafting from her now that she'd had an opportunity for the weight of her new knowledge to settle onto her.

"Are you certain, Rylan? I've never seen sparks that color. If there hasn't been an Ergokin in a millennia, how can you know it is my blessing?"

Rylan's eyes widened. Not due to her questioning his reading of the sparks. No. It was in utter shock that she saw varying colors in the sparks at all. Only Glassmakers were supposed to have the gift of seeing the kaleidoscope of colors produced during the shaping process.

"Sweeting, how do you know the color of the sparks?"

Chapter Five

Ophelia stared at Rylan with a wide-eyed expression she felt matched his own. He acted as if the flickers of light produced during the shaping of the glass weren't there for all to see. Surely she wasn't the only one who'd seen them other than him.

"I saw them, Rylan. As did everyone there. As did everyone who's ever watched a Glassmaker form a piece and render a blessing."

The shock on Rylan's face prompted Ophelia to seek her brothers. Although only two were near enough to have heard their conversation, she looked to them to validate her statement. However, instead of the confirmation she sought, incredulous looks were all she found.

"Sweeting...I have only ever known Glassmakers to be able to see and read the sparks."

Shaking her head, Ophelia shifted on the soft bedding Rylan gave her. That couldn't be right. Today hadn't been the first time she'd seen the colorful lights during the Glassmaker's reading. Her head swam with the new information and she struggled to accept his words.

"No, Rylan. I've always been able to see them." Despite their shocked expressions, she turned to her brothers. "Jaime, Kieran, you see them too. Right?"

"No, Phely. I've only ever seen bright lights when the Glassmaker reads the sparks. When it was my time, I didn't even see my own."

Ophelia swung her gaze to Kieran following Jaime's reply. Her youngest brother shrugged as he mirrored Jaime's words.

"So, what does that mean? Is that an ability of the Ergokin?"

Still not feeling as though she could confidently associate herself with the blessed group, Ophelia asked the question as if she was on the outside looking in. Being a part of such a rare group was far too much for her to acknowledge in such a short span of time.

"I can't say." Rylan's expression, while still tinged with awe, was softer. She could practically feel him willing her to calm herself. However, he didn't shy away from telling her what he did know about the blessing.

"From what was passed to me by my father and his father before him, was that the Ergokin blessing comes with the ability to control all forms of energy. Since every living thing has, or experiences a sort of energy, it means Ergokin can use their ability to amplify the blessings given to others.

Properly trained, an Ergokin can also stunt or mute the blessing of others. As I said before, energy is present in all things. It can't be destroyed, but an Ergokin can channel energy in whatever way and transform it into another shape at will."

They spoke the same language. Ophelia was sure she'd been able to understand each individual word he said. But, when she put them together in her mind, they twisted and realigned into something completely foreign. Because, there was no way this Glassmaker could be correct. If he was, it meant her blessing had truly manifested long before now.

She had memories of sitting on her father's shoulders watching the Glassmaker shape pieces, and declare the blessings of others prior to when she was presented to learn of her own. Even then, she'd marveled at the pretty rainbow of colors shooting out from the heated glass.

Rylan plucked her from her memory with a question which made her feel he could read her very thoughts.

"Do you recall how many winters you were when you first began to see the colors of the sparks?"

Slowly shaking her head, Ophelia looked down at her hands. "As far back as I can remember, I could always see them."

Tears pricked the back of Ophelia's eyes and she tried to keep them at bay. Winter after winter, she'd felt the weight of the prediction made by the Enchantress. When all this time, her blessing flowed through her. Had she used it unknowingly? Those who weren't mentored and trained properly on the use of their blessing could be a danger to themselves and everyone around them.

Had she unwittingly harmed someone with her wild, unchecked blessing? She didn't even know how it worked in order to prevent adverse results. Just as she was losing her battle with her emotions, Rylan's large, calloused hand covered hers.

"Sweeting, all will be okay. We will see the Keeper and she will know how to guide you. She will have the answer for both of us."

Sniffling, Ophelia lifted her gaze to Rylan's. His ruggedly handsome face was near hers allowing her to see the golden flecks in his emerald green eyes. His confidence served as a balm bolstering her ability to rein in her emotions. However, his statement brought up a new question.

"What answers do you need from the Keeper?"

"I have been a Glassmaker for this village for almost twenty winters, but today was the first time I was able to see the colors of someone's blessing *before* I ever read the sparks. I need to speak to her to understand it."

His admission surprised Ophelia. She'd met numerous Glassmakers over the revolutions, but she hadn't known any personally. She assumed their ability to read the sparks was a blessing, but she didn't know how it worked, and had no one to consult as to how that particular blessing manifested. Rylan wasn't just any Glassmaker though.

She didn't require a foresight blessing to know there was something special about him. After all, he'd been the only Glassmaker to make it to the point of proclaiming her blessing. Being presented to nearly every one of his kind in the realm was a testament to his uniqueness.

Ophelia cast her eyes down at their hands joined together in her lap. Her level of ease with the physical contact and being so near to him was another mystery. This one, she wasn't sure she was ready to solve. Lying just beneath the surface of her confusion regarding being Ergokin was an awareness of Rylan as a male. A large, virile looking, male who made no secret of his affection for her.

She couldn't fathom the source of his immediate familiarity with her. Beyond what Kieran had said earlier about their bond. Her serious suitors up to now were essentially non-existent, but her lack of experience with males had never bothered her. She'd had no desire to mate and bind her life to another's. Being so close to Rylan. With his masculine scent in her nose and heat wafting from his large frame, Ophelia wondered if she'd made an error in not paying more attention to mating customs beyond the talks her mother gave her when she had her first female courses.

In an attempt to redirect her thoughts to push down the

new wakefulness, she squeezed his fingers offering encouragement.

"The Keeper is the repository of our realm's knowledge. I'm confident she will have answers."

Lifting their joined hands, Rylan pressed his lips to the back of hers.

"Yes, Sweeting. She will."

Kieran cleared his throat loudly. Then, scant sands later, Damien and Ramo walked back into the small clearing leading their mounts. Wiggling her fingers, Ophelia attempted to disentangle them from Rylan's. He frowned his displeasure, but released her. However, he remained where he was with his large body folded next to hers.

Passing the reigns off to Ramo, Damien walked closer to the unlit fire pit staring at Ophelia and Rylan. His thoughts were written across his features.

"Glassmaker."

Rylan turned his attention to her older brother.

"Leander."

"You have been very helpful, and we appreciate it. But my sister isn't your reward for being useful. You're being too familiar with an unmated female."

Ophelia gasped in shock. Damien had said nothing in the workshop when Rylan placed himself between her and Caspian. Nor had he uttered a word when Rylan called her Sweeting. Yet, now he had words for the Glassmaker?

Despite the reprimand in her brother's tone, Rylan didn't move a muscle. Ophelia wasn't sure if she was impressed or frightened. Damien was rarely challenged. She considered shifting away on her own, but at the first tilt of her body, a low grunt came from Rylan. Without thought, she stopped fidgeting.

"What you consider too familiar, I consider offering comfort, Leander."

"Why would our sister require comfort? Did you do or say something to cause her pain?"

"Damien—" Ophelia attempted to put a stop to whatever was happening before it went too far.

"No, Sweeting. It is fine. Your brother is only concerned about your well-being." Patting her hand, Rylan stood to his full height, but didn't move away from her.

"I would never intentionally hurt Ophelia. She has learned a great deal today and was understandably concerned about what it all meant for her. I was simply explaining what I could to ease her mind."

"I'm not a sapling, and I have eyes. State your intentions toward my sister."

Ophelia hopped to her feet. She knew exactly what Damien was doing now. He was trying to force Rylan's hand. Jaime's announcement was fresh in her mind, but she had no intention of mentioning it to the Glassmaker. What was meant to be would come to pass without Damien shoving them toward acknowledging it.

"Damien! Stop it!"

The heat of Rylan's palm covered Ophelia's shoulder. Looking up at him, he simply shook his head to ask her to remain quiet.

Chapter Six

Rylan gently squeezed Ophelia's shoulder. Her brother's sudden line of questioning didn't bother him. Considering their protectiveness toward her, he was amazed it hadn't happened the first time he touched her.

"It's okay, Sweeting. Your brother is simply doing what brothers do. You cannot fault him for it."

Ophelia's beautiful face was scrunched in irritation. Rylan was barely able to control the desire to kiss her forehead to smooth away the expression. It didn't take a Diviner to tell him such an action wouldn't be well received. Returning his attention to the eldest Leander, Rylan released a slow breath.

He'd known from the moment he'd touched Ophelia that there was a special bond between the two of them. When he was willing to hitch up his wagon and see her to the Keeper personally, he conceded he didn't want their time together to end. There was only one way for a male to proceed under those circumstances.

"My intentions are to speak to the Leander patriarch to seek Ophelia's hand in the mating bond. I'd hoped to have time for us to get to know one another, and seek her permission before doing so. But, it appears that won't come to pass."

Rylan caught the glint of mischief in the other man's eyes before he hid it behind a stern expression.

"At the pace we're traveling, we should reach our village in three and a half rotations. Maybe four. You have until then to convince us."

"Convince you? Are you the Leander Patriarch?"

"No, but you should ask Ophelia what happened to her previous suitors. Didn't it seem strange to you that she's unmated after so many winters?"

Rylan shrugged. "I don't question gifts from the goddess. I simply appreciate them."

A grunt was the only reply from Damien. The other brothers followed his lead as they got themselves settled and discussed cycles for providing protection while their group slept. Although he doubted they trusted him enough to allow him a watch, Rylan volunteered anyway.

Ophelia situated herself on the nest of bedding he'd laid out for her. She'd acquiesced to his request to allow him to handle her brother, but her amber eyes blazed as she shot daggers at her siblings. Neither of them appeared fazed by her expression of discontent. Rylan would hazard to guess they were accustomed to it.

Damien's implication that the reason she remained unmated was due to something her brothers had done, meant they'd likely been on the receiving end of her wrath more than a few times. His Sweeting was beautiful and alluring. It was impossible she hadn't had numerous males attempt to gain her hand in mating. Thank the goddess they hadn't been successful.

Leaving his mats folded over, Rylan moved them closer to Ophelia. Under the watchful eyes of the Leander brothers, he sat on the folded bedding. He wasn't exactly sure how to steer the conversation back to what they were discussing before. Having lost even the semblance of privacy, he knew whatever they discussed could become a group conversation.

"Sweeting, do you mind telling me about your life in your village?" Rylan determined the question was safe enough.

After giving her brothers one last slit-eyed glare, Ophelia gave him her attention.

"Are we not going to discuss what you just said to Damien?"

"Is it necessary to do that now, Sweeting? We have long rotations ahead of us to explore any number of topics."

One finely arched brow lifted as she stared at him. "So, we are just to pretend you didn't propose a mating?"

"No. I meant what I said, but we are still new to each other. I think our time is better spent learning about one another's lives than discussing the wish my heart made when I first saw you."

Ophelia's skeptical gaze softened. Rylan hadn't meant to reveal so much, but he wouldn't retract the words. They were true. His heartbeat had never thundered for a female the way it did for his Sweeting from the very first instant he'd seen her. The most adorable flush crept into her rounded cheeks and she dipped her head shyly.

"My life in Misthaven isn't exciting. I mainly help my parents with their needs, and mind my nieces and nephews when my brothers and their mates need a break."

"So, all of your brothers are mated?"

"All except Kieran."

Ophelia bobbed her head tossing a glance at her brother who lay on his back eating dried meat with one hand, and petting his mount with the other. The horse nuzzled his arm when Kieran tried to stop stroking the white patch covering the center of the beast's head from between its ears to the tip of its muzzle.

The two of them spent considerable time discussing what she'd called her boring life. Rylan listened, wondering if she realized how intricately she was entwined in the daily fabric of her family. He also pondered if her father would be willing to accept him as her mate. While his status as Glassmaker was thought of highly in the realm, Rylan made his home many rotations journey away from Misthaven.

Her loss would be greatly felt were she to leave the village behind. Even if he considered joining her there, it was unheard of for two Glassmakers to inhabit the same village. The only time it occurred was during apprenticeship. Once a Glassmaker was deemed ready, they ventured out to make their homes elsewhere. His own father had many winters left as a Glassmaker. So, Rylan staying in the village of his birth hadn't been an option when he'd completed his time as his father's apprentice.

Without a fire and a Luminary, once the sun disappeared completely from the sky, the stars didn't light the night enough for them to continue talking. Reluctantly, Rylan moved his mats farther away from Ophelia—but not before attempting to convince her to sleep in the covered wagon.

As he thought she would, she declined. The wagon wasn't just protection from the night air, it also afforded more privacy since the cover was constructed of wood and metal. There wasn't a thin cloth barrier casting shadows from the light of lanterns.

Under the watchful gaze of the night sky, Rylan fell into a light doze contemplating what the next few rotations would bring. His concern for Ophelia wasn't unfounded. A Glassmaker never turned anyone away who came seeking to learn their blessing, but not all who left him with the knowledge were beings Rylan would've chosen to receive such precious gifts. Caspian Ironshade was one such being. Every unit of

Rylan's intuition said the possibility of securing an Ergokin was too tempting for Caspian to simply walk away.

When he'd *collected* the blessed previously it was through kinship or in trade for use of his vast lands. Those beings seemed content, but none had Ophelia's potential. It was simple to convince them to bind themselves to the wealthy male. However, a shrewd male such as Caspian would know he had no leverage with which to persuade Ophelia to join him willingly.

From their mounts, to their well-crafted attire, it was evident that the Leanders weren't in need of coin. With four strapping sons and a daughter skilled beyond her blessing, Rylan would be shocked to learn the family didn't have vast possessions of their own. If those things were apparent to *him*, Rylan had no doubt Caspian would swiftly reach the same conclusion.

They needed to get Ophelia to safety as soon as possible. Although he didn't have a designated time to sit watch, Rylan didn't fall into a deep sleep. Each time one of the brother's moved, he opened his eyes to watch the change of guard. His Sweeting slept through it all and rose with the sun wearing a smile, as she greeted the new rotation.

Once they completed their morning cleanliness routines, they had a breakfast of cold meat and some berries Damien found. After which, they mounted their horses and continued their journey. This time, Ramo trailed behind with Jaime riding beside Ophelia. Rylan had noticed their trail was almost undetectable. With the number of horses and his wagon, he questioned how they were so adept in concealing it.

He learned that where Damien was a Seeker, Ramo was a Qarikin. Although he hadn't encountered many, Rylan knew how fortunate they were to have one among them. Qarkins could obscure anything they didn't want found. Only a very talented Seeker could discover what a Qarikin wanted hidden.

So, following the markings of their steeds and the wagon wheels was unlikely.

Which left the alternative of a Changer. Since he'd been Glassmaker at Thistledown, Rylan hadn't read the blessing of a Changer. However, it didn't mean there wasn't one in Caspian's cohort. With a Changer's capability to take on the form of animals, they also enjoyed the abilities of the creature they mimicked. So, while their physical trail may be undetectable, their scents carried on the wind. Rylan wasn't sure even a strong Qarikin could prevent that.

Chapter Seven

They'd kept a grueling pace for the past two rotations and Ophelia was barely able to sit on her mount. Her own fatigue coupled with her knowledge that Starlight wasn't accustomed to such long journeys without rest drove her to accept Rylan's repeated requests for her to join him in the wagon. He graciously offered his mount to her brothers to allow them to give their own mount's rest.

Unfortunately, only Jaime was deemed acceptable by Shadowfox. So, her other brothers switched between the horses they'd brought with them. They considered Starlight too small for them, so she was tethered to the rear of the wagon while she rested.

As much as Ophelia tried to remain upright and discourage physical contact between herself and Rylan, weariness soon won out. Starting their rotation with the sun and not stopping until the moon appeared had taken its toll. She was answering one of his numerous questions when she felt herself tilt, landing against his side with her head resting on his meaty upper arm.

Before she could succumb to embarrassment, she was

asleep. Much later, the motion of the wagon went from a gentle sway to jostling, jarring Ophelia awake. With wide eyes, she sat up straight trying to make sense of what was happening.

"Sweeting, I need you to climb into the back of the wagon." Rylan's naturally deep voice had an urgent edge to it.

"What's going on?" Sleep still had a slight hold on Ophelia keeping her from immediately assessing her surroundings.

"Riders are coming. Ramo doesn't think they're friendly. It's best if you aren't seen. There is no time to waste, Sweeting. I need you to get in back now."

Not questioning him further, Ophelia balanced herself against Rylan as she climbed into the covered portion of the wagon.

"Go back farther."

Rylan bit out the instruction when she perched on the end of the bench only a foot behind where he sat.

"I know how to defend myself, Rylan. I don't have to hide."

Keeping his attention on guiding the wagon on the barely worn trail, Rylan replied, "I have no doubt you can, Sweeting. But I won't have you in harm's way. Save your strength for when it's absolutely necessary for you to fight."

Moving as far back into the wagon as she could go without exiting the rear door, Ophelia sat on the top of a wooden chest. Holding on to the edge of the large box with one hand and the wagon wall with the other, she tried to keep herself steady. More than she wanted to know who their potential assailants were, she wished that she'd learned of her blessing sooner.

Having no idea how it worked or how to control it, she couldn't offer assistance beyond the fighting skills she'd learned from her papa and brothers. She knew Ramo had been using his blessing to hide their tracks, and wondered why that hadn't been enough. Why couldn't he hide them completely?

Ophelia couldn't see anything beyond the dark interior of the wagon, but she stared at the opposite wall envisioning her brothers riding their horses in tandem to keep the wagon at the center of protection. She could almost see Ramo as he focused his energy on using his gift. She could practically feel the waves bouncing around her.

The desire to do something, anything, welled inside her. Yielding to it, Ophelia invited the energy inside. Instinct told her to concentrate on Ramo. So, she did. Her focus was so singular, the sounds of their pursuers faded for a moment. When the volume returned to her surroundings, the thundering hooves were fading and the wagon had slowed. Once again, it swayed gently over the slightly worn path.

"What in the netherworld just happened?"

Damien's question reached Ophelia as she pried her fingers away from the edge of the chest. On shaking legs, she stood. With tentative steps, she walked toward the front of the wagon to peer out at her brothers. Five pair of eyes stared back at her. Each filled with awe.

"What?" Just as confused as her siblings, Ophelia held on to the wagon wall.

Unable to hold her up any longer, Ophelia's legs gave way depositing her on the edge of the bench. At least she blamed it on her limbs, and not the intensity of the way Rylan looked at her, and her inability to break away from his gaze.

"It was like they couldn't see us." Kieran looked from Ophelia to Ramo. "Did you do that?"

"If I did, I've never done it before." Ramo looked even more shocked than their other brothers. The only one who didn't look confused was Rylan.

"You did it with your sister's help." Rylan finally released her from his stare to speak to Ramo.

"Are you sure?" Ophelia could tell Damien's question stemmed from genuine curiosity.

"Yes. I felt the same feeling I had when I first began working the glass the rotation you brought her to me. I'd never felt anything like it. Once I realized she was Ergokin, it became clear what occurred."

When he spoke, Rylan looked back at Ophelia. She didn't fully understand it herself, so she listened as raptly as her siblings.

"Reading the sparks was simply confirmation of the colors I could see surrounding her the first moment I saw her. That hadn't been the way of things for me. At least not until a few rotations ago. After her, it was the same for the boy. She amplified my abilities. It was like a dam was washed away, or scales were removed from my eyes."

Ramo snapped his fingers. "That's exactly what it felt like. Like a dam bursting. Even though I could hear the riders approaching, I directed all of my energy toward keeping our trail hidden. Once they came into view, and I saw their numbers, I didn't just want to hide our tracks, I wanted to hide *us* completely.

Then, this feeling washed over me and it was like I was projecting—making the thing I wanted a reality. When I saw that they hadn't drawn weapons, I gained more confidence. The power was…"

Ramo trailed off as if he couldn't adequately complete his thought, but Rylan nodded in understanding. At least one of them could relate, because Ophelia remained in the dark. *Had she really amplified Ramo's blessing? Or, did he simply unlock the next level of it during a moment of crisis?*

If she had helped her brother, how? Was it when she allowed the energy pulsing around her to have a home then sent it out, directed at him? Is that the way of the Ergokin?

47

Weariness made her sway. Ophelia wasn't certain if it was due to the weightiness of the moment or mental exertion.

"Perhaps you should lie down, Sweeting. It might be best if we find a place to camp. Obscuring such a large number of people and creatures had to be taxing on both of you."

Apparently, Ophelia's body agreed on her behalf. A boneless feeling overtook her just before she felt Rylan's strong arm at her back gently guiding her to lie on the cushioned bench inside the wagon. Although the air wasn't cool, he draped a light blanket over her. Prior to sleep completely consuming her, she heard her brothers agree and the wagon rolled, lightly jostling her as it turned from the path.

The next time she opened her eyes, the night sky greeted her through the opening at the front of the wagon. Male voices, in hushed conversation, drifted to her ears as she turned to her side. Sitting up, she contemplated leaving the comfort of the bench, which was more like a small bed with the soft bedding Rylan had added. As if simply thinking of him caused him to appear, a head of dark hair and brilliant green eyes materialized at the edge of the wagon cover.

"Good. You're awake." The carriage swayed slightly under his weight as he climbed onto it.

"Your brother went down for a little while too. But he's up now as well. We still don't think it's safe to have a fire, but I brought you something to eat. You need to keep up your strength."

Ophelia watched Rylan from half-lowered lids. He hadn't struck her as a particularly verbose male, but he kept up his one-sided dialogue for a few moments before he quieted. He didn't enter the back of the wagon with her, but he didn't have to. His arms were long enough to reach her easily to pass the food he'd wrapped in a cloth for her.

"Come, Sweeting. Eat."

Ignoring the way her lady parts responded to the

command in his voice, Ophelia sat up farther. Tucking her legs beneath her, she accepted his offering. The night sky seemed to glow brighter casting a devastating glow around Rylan. Shyness stole over her, and Ophelia dropped her eyes to her lap concentrating on the modest dinner he provided.

Rylan was a Glassmaker, not a Spellcaster. Yet she felt as if there was a spell being woven around her when he gave her his undivided attention. Kieran's declaration came back to her then in full force. *"He is your mate."*

Goddess help her. The knowledge of their bond coupled with the way he sought to care for her made it impossible for her to resist the thrall dragging her closer to him with each rotation.

Chapter Eight

Rylan wished for more privacy with Ophelia, but knew it was best that they had their chaperones. Had they been alone, her innocence would be long forgotten. The instinctive pull he'd felt toward her, from their first meeting, intensified with each passing moment. It drove him to do whatever he could to be near her.

Never having a mate or more than passing dalliances with females didn't deter him. He had no idea what other males did in care for their mates, but Rylan was compelled to provide for his Sweeting in every way that was available for him. If it meant playing her lady's maid, so be it.

Earlier, when he'd thought he'd be forced to draw his weapons, his only thought had been about keeping her safe from harm. Not being a male bent on war didn't prevent him from desiring to stop the wagon and rend their pursuers limb from limb. Only the probability that they'd be vastly outnumbered by other blessed beings kept him from completely losing control.

The sheer number of beings on horses who passed them

by said his logical mind was correct. Had he given in to the urge to lay waste to the ones chasing them, it would've ended badly. He had no doubt he could defend her, but the streaks of colors surrounding the males indicated a variety of the blessed were in Caspian's cohort.

Snapping back into the present, Rylan watched as Ophelia ate the food he'd brought her. Her eldest brother Damien had once again found edible fruit nearby to add to the cured meats and bread. He'd also located a stream to secure fresh water. Once Ophelia was nearly done eating, Rylan decided to break the news to her surrounding their travel situation.

"Sweeting, we can no longer afford to only travel during the early rotation light. The going will be slower without the sun, but we have to keep moving. Ramo is only able to prevent us from being discovered for so long." When he saw her preparing to interject, he held up a hand.

"I know you could help him. But without real control, you both will likely end up over exerting yourselves. This way is better."

"But—"

"No, Sweeting. We've discussed it. The extent of your blessing is unknown to us. Do you really want to risk harming your brother by over taxing his blessing with yours?"

Ophelia's lips clamped shut, and Rylan felt a twinge of guilt. From their talks and interactions, doing nothing wasn't something she did well. He had a suspicion she would try, regardless of their wishes. With silence as her answer, he encouraged her to finish eating while he and her brothers set everything to rights so they could begin moving again. They'd have to adjust their route to hopefully avoid the small contingent.

Rylan was certain the males were Caspian's as they were wearing the Ironshade family colors and a few had the crest sewn onto their garments. For him, there was no doubt that the group was tracking Ophelia. So, the sooner they reached the relative safety of Misthaven, the better.

It didn't take long for them to restore the grounds to their previous condition, and it was like they were never there. Having Damien as a guide was perfect. The Seeker didn't need a well-traveled path to locate a way home. His blessing meant he could navigate them to their destination without following the normal roads. Although, things were sometimes rocky with the wagon, Rylan refused to leave it behind.

Thank the goddess, they didn't encounter Caspian's people again. By mid-rotation of the third sunrise since they'd left Rylan's workshop, the outline of Misthaven appeared in the distance. Now riding her mount once more, Ophelia sat higher in the seat. He watched her, mesmerized by the transformation of her features. Seeing her home caused her to radiate joy.

As they drew closer, he noticed the way people came from their homes to call out greetings to the Leanders. It seemed they were well known and liked in Misthaven. One of the reasons why became apparent when they stopped so the brothers could assist a widow dealing with a load much too heavy for one to handle alone. Waving off his offer of assistance, they set her carriage to rights and saw her the remainder of the way to her cottage.

Before they reached the village proper, they veered from the main road. All that could be seen ahead of them were green fields with tall trees in the distance. Nearer to the trees, the road inclined. It wasn't until they reached the top of the hill that Rylan had an idea of where they were going.

To him, the structure nestled in the valley between the green hills resembled a castle with two tall turrets and the remaining portion of it spread over a large area. It could likely accommodate Ophelia, her parents and siblings along with their mates and offspring. However, he was disabused of his thought by his Sweeting. She pointed to the moderately sized house in the near distance.

"There's where Jaime and his mate live. I don't see the younglings outside playing. So, his mate may have taken them to the main house with our parents."

Happy she was speaking to him again, Rylan nodded, then pointed to the next house he saw on the left.

"What about there?"

"Magnus and Valeria live there. They are kin by way of my uncle. Valeria is his daughter. They chose to live here on Leander land instead of near his family in Ravensworth. He and Valeria are both Earthers. We have them to thank for these sprawling fruitful fields."

Rylan nodded. He recalled one of the brothers mentioning the variety of blessed in the Leander line. Having Earthers meant their people would likely never go hungry. Ophelia continued to point out the inhabitants of the various dwellings as they got closer to the home she shared with her parents. When they reached a stone path leading to the entrance of what she'd called the main house, a tall broad-shouldered male stepped outside. His dark brown skin shown in the sunlight similar to Ophelia's. The male was at minimum her kin, but Rylan suspected he was her father.

Kicking her mount to a gallop, Ophelia shot ahead of the group. The brothers made room as if they'd known it would happen before her mount ever accelerated. Reaching the male, she hopped from her steed and was swept into a hug. As she was placed back on her feet, a female wearing a slightly older version of Ophelia's face came into view. Although she didn't sweep his Sweeting off her feet, she did wrap the younger female in a big hug as well.

By the time the rest of them made it into what Rylan dubbed a courtyard, their reunion was in full swing. One would think they'd been separated for revolutions instead of a handful of rotations. Their affection for one another was obvious, if somewhat foreign to him.

The same amber eyes the siblings bore stared at Rylan as he brought his wagon to a stop behind the brothers.

"Sons, is there something you need to tell me?" The elder Leander looked at them expectantly.

Damien spoke for the group. "This is the Glassmaker from Thistledown. He is called, Rylan. He was able to read the sparks, and tell us Phely's blessing."

The older female clasped her hands in front of her gasping, then she captured Ophelia in another hug. "What?! Why didn't you say anything? I knew it! I told your father we couldn't give up. The Enchantress wasn't wrong. You *are* blessed. Those other Glassmakers just didn't have the skills to see it."

Climbing down from his wagon, Rylan stepped forward extending his hand to the elder Leander.

"Rylan of the Sunweavers, and Glassmaker for Thistledown."

"Theron of the Leanders."

The older male grasped Rylan's forearm in a strong grip, greeting him in the customary way. While the male was likely at least twenty winters older than Rylan, his hold was formidable.

"Thank you for your service, Glassmaker."

"The honor is mine." Rylan nodded respectfully.

The Leander's mate waved her hands gesturing toward the large wooden doors.

"Come! Come inside! We have much to discuss!"

Looking behind him, Rylan noted a few young boys had appeared and were taking care of the horses. So, he followed the others inside. He barely glanced at the interior as his attention was entirely on Ophelia. Her previous joy had ebbed slightly, and she now appeared nervous. Without a thought to decorum, Rylan strode to her side.

"What's wrong, Sweeting?"

Chapter Nine

Ophelia's eyes rounded at Rylan's use of the endearment in front of her parents. When she'd first seen her father step out into the entryway of their home, she was ecstatic. She was equally happy to see her mother. Although she hadn't been gone for very long, she'd missed them. However, when Damien introduced Rylan, reality came crashing down.

Being able to face her parents with confirmation of a blessing should've felt wonderful. They'd prayed to the goddess, and consulted Diviners on her behalf for most of her life. As of four rotations ago, they could stop. The sparks had been read, and her blessing proclaimed.

Now what? The Enchantress hadn't given a guidebook as to how Ophelia's blessing would bring about the restoration of their family. So, the weight she thought would be lifted, had gotten heavier.

When she simply stared at him without answering, Rylan's brows dipped. His concern was unmistakable. The hands which shaped the vessels of blessings grasped her shoulders gently.

"Sweeting?"

As much as his touch was soothing, having him be so familiar in the presence of her parents was anxiety ridden. What would they think she'd done during the rotations she'd been away from them? The number of winters she'd seen didn't matter. She was an unmated female. Shaking her head at Rylan, Ophelia stepped away from his touch.

"I'm okay."

"No, daughter. You definitely are not." Her father's knowing expression matched her mother's. The two had been mated for so long, they sometimes seemed to share one mind.

Ophelia didn't want to argue with her father, but she also didn't want attention placed on her, Rylan, and their bond. There were other things to discuss. She knew there was no running from what Kieran said about her and Rylan. However, they'd traveled to Thistledown to have a Glassmaker read the sparks for her. They'd accomplished their task, and needed to relay to their parents all which ensued.

"I really am, Papa. Besides, you and Mama haven't heard about my blessing."

"Yeah..." Damien chimed in. "About that. It might be best if we sit for this part."

Her mother reached Ophelia's side sliding an arm around her waist.

"Why do you look so sad, Phely? I don't need to know what blessing the goddess gifted to you to know you're special. You always have been. So, why do I feel as though you'd prefer things as they were?"

Because I would... Ophelia kept her internal thought to herself. Instead, she laid her hand on her mother's where it rested above her hip.

"Let's go sit, Mama. We'll tell you everything."

Never far away, Ophelia felt Rylan's presence at her back as she walked through the arched doorway into the next room. It was the space where they typically gathered as a family. The hearth was so large, she could almost stand up straight inside. Once they were all seated, Ophelia took her mother's hand and stared between her parents.

"Can you tell me what you know about Ergokin?"

Her mother's eyes widened, and one hand flew to her mouth as she gasped.

"Ergokin? You're Ergokin?" Not giving Ophelia a chance to answer her question, she turned to her husband, sharing her astonishment. "She's Ergokin, Theron. Has there been an Ergokin in living memory?"

"No. Not that I recall. We'd have to ask the Chronicler. But I believe it's been more than two millennia since the last Ergokin was born."

His voice was softer than usual. It gave the impression he was answering automatically, which meant his thoughts were racing. Ophelia learned over the revolutions that when her father spoke in low, soft tones, he was thinking. It would appear he was barely listening, but he'd respond this way until he'd come to a conclusion in his mind. Only then would he return to his normal speech pattern.

Ophelia's mother, Aria, wasn't paying attention to her husband's distracted response. She had her answer, and set into gushing chatter about how the blessing confirmed what she'd always known. She even affirmed that she'd known Ophelia would be special from the moment of her conception.

Being the youngest of their five younglings, Ophelia often wondered if the reason they had five younglings was because one or both of her parents were determined to be the progenitor of the female youngling the Enchantress spoke of. Ophelia was certain her mother would've continued with her mini celebration had her father not put an end to it by speaking to Damien.

"Son, there is more to tell. Speak." Her father's normal baritone had returned, which meant he'd come to a conclusion. In his time, he would tell them. But not until he was ready.

Clearing his throat, Damien looked from his father to Ophelia then to Rylan. Afterwards, he launched into the recounting of the events following the reading of the sparks. During the retelling, her mother grasped her hands tugging Ophelia close as if Caspian was going to storm through their front door and snatch her away. When Damien was done, her father shook his head gravely.

"With every great blessing, evil is always present." Patting his wife's shoulder, her father stood. He paced in front of the unlit fireplace.

"All the revolutions spent with Glassmakers unable or unwilling to try to read the sparks for Ophelia, when my confidence in the prophecy should've faded, I became even more convinced that whatever her blessing, it would come with great change. Knowing greatness attracts the best and worst of the goddess's beings, I've been preparing for a time such as this."

Ophelia was comforted in knowing her papa had prepared for the possibility of someone like Caspian, but concerned about the cost to be paid for those who stood beside them. Her brothers' relief was much more visible than her own. As the eldest son himself, their father was accustomed to leading and leaders had to have a vision.

Her gaze traveled around the room, her eyes cataloguing everyone's demeanor and response. When she reached Rylan, his eyes were waiting for hers. The intensity of his stare hadn't waned. If anything, it was stronger. His determination was written in the set of his jaw and tension in his shoulders. He only broke his stare when her father asked him a question directly.

"How do you fit into all of this, Glassmaker? I appreciate you alerting my younglings to potential danger, and agreeing to travel with them to see the Keeper. But, I'm not without sight. I know there's more to your presence here than the quest for knowledge and drive to do what's right."

Standing to his full height, Rylan met her father's stare head on. Ophelia's insides flipped at his calm, self-assured carriage. Then, dread twisted into a knot in her belly. Rylan had already proven he wasn't one to mince words. Having been asked a direct question, he'd give a direct answer. Her breath was trapped in her lungs, as she watched the interchange that would likely further alter her life.

"I don't fully understand it, but I have a connection with Ophelia. I *did* volunteer to bring her to the Keeper to help her with her blessing, but also because mine appears to be tied to hers."

"Is that all?"

Ophelia tried not to cringe at the bite in her father's question.

"No, sir. It's not. Beyond the connection of our blessings, I'm drawn to her. The time spent traveling from Thistledown, getting the opportunity to talk with her, it has served to strengthen that draw."

"Speak plainly, Glassmaker."

"I believe she is my mate. The one the goddess created for me as she created me for her. I couldn't stay in Thistledown as she traveled the roads leading away from me and into certain danger."

Ophelia's heart raced during the entire exchange. Her fingers were clamped together in her lap as her mother squeezed her shoulders anchoring her in the moment. This would be the second time Rylan had stated his desire to be her mate in front of her family. Without anyone telling him of the mate bond Kieran could see tying them together, Rylan was declaring it boldly.

Her racing heart was sent into overdrive with utter shock

when her papa didn't immediately deny Rylan's claim. While he'd allowed her brothers to handle potential suitors in the past, she'd seen him glare at young males who thought to approach her in the market. When he did look to her brothers, it was to Kieran specifically.

Not missing anything in the nonverbal conversation, Ophelia saw Kieran's chin dip in an almost imperceptible nod. His acknowledgement of the truth of Rylan's claim didn't seem to please their father. His face closed up making his expression unreadable.

"Aria, my heart. I'm sure Phely is hungry, tired, and wants to wash away the dust from the road. Would you take her to her rooms and help her?"

What?! Heat surged up Ophelia's spine. Was her father really dismissing her while there was an active discussion about *her* going on?

"I'm fine, Papa. I can stay." Taking a chance, she squared her shoulders, sitting up straight next to her mother.

"Sweeting."

It wasn't him using the term of endearment which melted Ophelia's resolve. It was the way he said the word that had her acquiescing. Shooting him a glance projecting her thoughts, she stood with her mother. His responding nod said her message was received. He'd tell her everything later.

Chapter Ten

"I never thought I'd see such." The normally silent Jaime spoke dryly once Ophelia and her mother left the room.

"You? Brother, I could see the top ready to pop on her kettle." Ramo added incredulously.

"That's enough." Theron Leander stared at Rylan as he spoke to his sons. His penetrating gaze would've caused a lesser male to shrink and fumble in the simple act of breathing, but Rylan just waited for what was to come.

Nothing the other male said would change what he knew to be true. Ophelia was his mate. Instinct led him to attach himself to her, but the full understanding of why, hit him squarely between the eyes when her father began to question him. At that moment, Rylan knew simply requesting her hand or permission to court her would never be enough.

Not when he longed to do more than look upon her beauty. Not when the desire to touch her and physically bind them together was so strong, he wasn't certain he wouldn't spirit her away the moment they were on their way to see the Keeper.

"I can see from your confidence, you believe what you just

said is the truth. Lucky for you, Kieran confirms it. But it doesn't mean I'll simply hand my only daughter over to you. No matter what the fates have told you about a *connection* between you, I'm her father. I will protect her and see that she's protected when I'm not there to do it myself."

Since he hadn't asked a question, Rylan stood silently listening. He didn't blame the elder Leander. If, and when, he had a daughter, he wouldn't simply turn her over to a male who showed up claiming to be her mate. However, understanding the other male's perspective, didn't mean Rylan would cower at the implication of potentially having to suffer his wrath. Rylan would do that and so much more for his Sweeting.

"No matter the bond the two of you have, it doesn't mean you'll be able to provide for her and protect her the way she deserves. Ophelia is special. Beyond the blessing of being Ergokin, she lives under a prophecy which foretold of her birth three generations ago."

Anger simmered in Rylan's gut when Theron implied he couldn't protect or provide for Ophelia. Not a prideful or boastful male, Rylan knew he was gifted in a sea of the gifted. Although profit was never his goal, being a Glassmaker had stocked his coffers, and his own holdings weren't small. But, he was certain the Leander's biggest concern was the public lifestyle most Glassmakers lead.

Being the proclaimer of blessings meant there would always be visitors, some of them strangers, at his home or workshop. If it became common knowledge that his mate possessed such a rare blessing, it would require measures a Glassmaker didn't normally have to take to secure their family's safety. There would be those, like Caspian who would covet such a person, and be uncaring of the status the Glassmaker held.

Instead of allowing his anger to rule him, Rylan leaned

against the mantle of the large fireplace and crossed his arms over his chest. He'd wait to see what else the Leander had to say before he spoke on any of it.

"While my father was still in his mother's womb, his parents went to the Enchantress in Ravensworth at her request. She'd seen a vision of a girl youngling born to our people. She said the youngling would possess magicks not seen in generations, and she would restore the Leander line.

Until Ophelia's birth there hadn't been a female born into the family in seven generations, and only three since. The others weren't born until after the first time we presented Ophelia to the Glassmaker at five winters old. When he said he had no blessing for her, then the other female younglings were born. They thought maybe the prophecy was for them. I didn't believe it was so. I was certain it was for my youngling. When each of them went to the Glassmaker and the sparks declared their very common blessings, my resolve was renewed. Now, after all of these winters, my faith has been confirmed. However, the result brings with it understandable fear for Ophelia."

Concern for Ophelia's well-being was a subject on which Rylan and the Leander could both agree. He'd yet to officially claim her anywhere but his mind, but Rylan knew he would wreak havoc should one hair on her beautiful head be harmed. His proclamation to her family was just that, until they were bound together in a union.

Listening to the story, he also now understood the hint of sadness he detected in his Sweeting's eyes when she learned of her blessing. The knowledge confirmed a burden which would be heavy for even the strongest of beings.

When the other male was silent for a stretch, Rylan decided to ask a question burning his mind from the moment the prophecy was mentioned.

"The Enchantress said the Leander line would be restored.

As we entered the area near Misthaven, it appeared to me that your family is well thought of by those who inhabit the village. This home you live in is as grand a castle as I've seen. And from what was explained to me as we drew near this towering structure, the land surrounding it belongs to the Leanders. What is left to restore?

You have five offspring. All of whom have received blessings from the goddess. Your fields have bountiful crops, and your livestock look healthy and plentiful. There are many living within the realm who are not nearly as fortunate as the Leanders."

Rylan's question was genuine. Although he was born into a long line of Glassmakers, and they were revered for being the conduit through which the goddess rendered her blessings, not all of them had the possessions or the genuine acceptance from villages they served.

Something flashed across the Leander's face before he closed it up once more. However, instead of the wall of silence Rylan expected, the Leander walked to a tapestry hanging from one of the walls. Running his fingers across the intricate design featuring a lion and a dragon engaged in battle, he started to speak.

"Several generations ago, one of my ancestors was entered into a mating oath with a Firefist. The mating would unite our two powerful families. The Leanders were traditionally Changers who favored the lion form. The Firefists were also traditionally Changers. They favored the Wyvern."

Rylan noticed the way the brothers all leaned toward their father and wondered if they'd ever actually heard the story he'd begun to tell.

"Our family had been in Willowmere for more than three centuries forging alliances. We were well respected. Then the eldest Leander daughter reached mating age, and the unthinkable happened. She petitioned her father to break the oath with the Firefists, because she'd fallen in love with another. She wanted to mate for love and not alliances. The male she loved was a Dragon Changer from the Bloodraven line.

Despite having the confirmation of a Soulkin that their mating was true and destined, the Firefists didn't want to release her from the oath made by her father. When her father wouldn't force her, the Firefists said the Leanders were a family without honor. They were willing to go to war over it, and did.

By the end, almost all of the Firefists were gone, but the damage had been done to the Leander name. We were seen as oath breakers and slaughterers. The daughter also lost her mate in battle. The Leanders were ostracized. The Bloodravens no longer wanted to align themselves with our family. We were no longer respected citizens of Willowmere. So, the patriarch made the decision to relocate the family to this part of the realm and start over.

But it was as if we were cursed. From that point on, not one girl youngling was born to the Leanders until Ophelia's birth. We had to become self-sufficient as word had spread even so far away from Willowmere, and there weren't many who wanted to align themselves with oath breakers."

Chapter Eleven

Rylan listened to the Leander detail what he considered his family's shame without comment. He stared at the tapestry. Closer inspection showed the lion and the dragon woven into the fabric weren't fighting one another. They each held pieces of another creature in their claws. Focusing on that area, he realized each had the webbed arm of a wyvern in their clawed grasp.

The older male ran his fingers along that area of the wall-hanging as if he knew it had drawn Rylan's attention. However, he'd never turned to look at anyone else while he spoke.

"This was crafted as a reminder. For the ancestral daughter, it was a tribute to her love for the mate she'd lost. For me, it is a cautionary tale. The Bloodravens didn't suffer as the Leanders did. Their loss wasn't as great and they weren't viewed as harshly as our family.

As a father myself, I know I wouldn't force my Phely to mate with anyone she was unwilling to bind her life to. My brothers and I were the first generation to not encounter as many barriers to pursuing mates. I have my suspicion that it had something to do with the prophecy. To receive it was an honor other families wanted to be a part of.

So, what you saw on your way here was the result of over two hundred revolutions of hard work and matings made in the hopes of being able to claim a double-blessed youngling as a member of their bloodline."

Rylan was thankful for the additional insight. Coming from a line of Glassmakers, he understood the Leander's perspective on mating. Before he'd completed his apprenticeship, there were females being pressed toward him by their mothers. Not because they saw Rylan as a mate who would protect and provide for their daughters, but because of the way they viewed Glassmakers and their position in society.

However, Rylan wasn't like some other Glassmakers. He didn't allow the adulation to define him. He simply used his blessing and hoped he was doing it as the goddess intended.

That being said, he understood the concept of being coveted as a mate for the wrong reasons. The concern Ophelia's father had was legitimate. But, Rylan wouldn't be deterred from claiming the female who'd been crafted specifically for him—no matter who thought to keep them apart. Finally looking away from the intricate tapestry, Rylan allowed his gaze to roam around the room looking at each male present.

"I cannot fathom having to deal with the things your family has endured. My life as a Glassmaker and the son of a Glassmaker has been one of elevated privilege. I won't deny it. My only hardship has been moving away to start my own life in Thistledown. That in itself wasn't as difficult due to my skill with the forge and reading the sparks.

Physical comforts notwithstanding, it doesn't mean I am a soft male who doesn't have the strength or means to keep Ophelia safe nor the capability of providing for her other needs. Until my last breath, my charge will be to keep her in the life she deserves using whatever means necessary to accomplish the task."

Rylan didn't have to hear either of the Leanders say it. None of them wanted to turn Ophelia over to any man—let alone one they had no knowledge of until less than a moon cycle ago. Dropping his arms to his sides, he assumed a more open posture.

"What assurances are required for you to know my word is true? Is there a quest? The blessing of a Soulkin? A bride price?"

Having never attempted to court a female, Rylan wasn't sure of the procedure, but he'd do whatever was necessary to make certain that Ophelia was bound to him as his mate before the end of the next moon cycle. Sooner, if possible.

Shaking his head, the Leander lifted a hand brushing away Rylan's suggestions.

"There is no need for a quest, and my family doesn't hold to tradition with bride prices and dowries. What is hers goes with Ophelia no matter who she chooses to mate. But it is *her* choice. As for a Soulkin..." He looked from Rylan to Kieran.

"Kieran is Soulkin."

Rylan assessed Ophelia's brother with new eyes. He was the brother closest to Ophelia in age, but he still hadn't seen as many winters as Rylan. None of the brothers had. Rylan studied Kieran briefly before returning his stare to Theron Leander.

"Have you told me this because your son has already confirmed my mate bond with Ophelia?"

He assumed it had to be the case. Otherwise, why would the Leander go through the trouble of expounding on their family history and indulging Rylan's questions about the restoration of their family line? The other male turned the same dark golden eyes, that he'd passed to each of his offspring, onto Rylan.

"Yes. He has seen it. His blessing hasn't led anyone astray from his first declaration. So, I believe him."

The Leander's voice still had a trace of sadness undergirded by a steel resolve. "That doesn't mean I'm okay with simply putting my daughter into the hands of a virtual stranger."

Standing taller, Rylan met the older male's determined stare with one of his own.

"I may be a stranger to you, but Ophelia knows me. Your sons know me. It may have only been a few rotations, but I have shown them nothing which would make me unfit to be your daughter's mate. And as you've just said, a Soulkin you trust, your son, has confirmed what I've felt from the moment I saw her.

Ophelia is *my* mate. Our lives are tethered to one another's for the rest of our rotations here in this realm. All that is left is to officially declare it before the goddess and our families. Given the current situation, I am okay with not having my family present for the ceremony."

Low chuckles drew Rylan's attention to Ramo who sat to Kieran's left with mirth dancing in his eyes. Soon, the others joined him regarding Ramo's now, boisterous, amusement. When everyone's gaze was on him, but they didn't join in his glee, his laughter faded.

"What?...Wait, he's serious? He wants to have the mating ceremony immediately?"

"That's what it sounds like," Damien said dryly.

To Rylan's ear, he didn't sound enthused at the possibility, but Rylan couldn't give two skat piles. He had the confirmation of a Soulkin that his heart was correct about Ophelia. There was no time like the present to make things official. What would be the point of waiting? To put on a show for others? Such a thing was wholly unnecessary to Rylan. But, if his Sweeting wanted it.

Contemplating Ophelia's want for their joining ceremony prompted a question. Turning to Kieran again, Rylan studied him once more.

"Does your sister know? Did you tell *her* what you saw?"

Kieran's gaze flicked to his father's before returning to Rylan's. With a nod, he confirmed it.

"When? How long has she known?" Other than when he was gathering his supplies and hitching his horse to his carriage, they hadn't been apart.

"She's known since before we left Thistledown."

Chapter Twelve

Ophelia allowed her mother to hustle her from the room with the males and into her suite. She wasn't given much of an option to protest or ask questions as she was stripped naked and assisted into the large clawfoot bathing tub by her mother and a couple young ladies who helped around the keep. Ophelia didn't like to refer to them as servants. Some of them were almost as close as family.

However, no matter how fondly she viewed the young ladies, she didn't utter a word about her blessing, the aftermath of the Glassmaker reading the sparks, and definitely didn't mention Rylan by name. At least, not until she and her mother were alone.

Sitting on the tufted bench in front of the mirror, Ophelia brushed a section of her long coily strands while her mother stood on her other side working cream into another section. The scene was similar to when she was a young girl. Only then, Ophelia had to be chased and practically tied to the seat to sit through the exercise.

"So, your Glassmaker is a bold one, daughter. But, I should have known the male the goddess crafted for you wouldn't be some shrinking bundle of nerves unable to stake his claim."

"He's not my Glassmaker, Mama."

Her mother's fingers stilled. "That's not what he said, and I'm positive I heard him clearly. And the fact Kieran didn't immediately refute his statement says he's right."

Their gazes connected in the reflection in the glass. "Are you saying he is dreaming and your brother's blessing led him astray?"

"No, Mama." Ophelia paused dropping the hand holding the brush to her lap. "I'm saying, him believing us to be mates and Kieran's ability to see the mate bond, doesn't mean he's mine."

Dropping her hands to Ophelia's shoulders, her mother squeezed. "My dear, that's exactly what it means. Whether you are ready to accept it or not, he is the male the goddess has tied your life to. Could you mate with someone else and be happy? Possibly. But, accepting the Glassmaker ensures the additional blessing of the goddess on your union. It makes for an unbreakable bond. So, yes. He's *your* Glassmaker."

Since it was pointless to argue with her mother, Ophelia lifted the brush and went back to detangling her hair. Meanwhile, her mother continued to chatter. Ophelia was certain it was partially to try to keep her occupied and not rushing back down to the main hall to find out what was happening between Rylan, her father, and her brothers.

Part of her was still fuming that she'd been asked to leave the room while her future was deliberated as if she was some addle-headed ninny who had no brain function. If her future was being discussed, why couldn't she participate in the conversation?

"I will say this, Phely. Your Glassmaker is one fine specimen of maleness. He must do more than work the forge to garner such muscles. I would've thought him a warrior or blacksmith if Damien hadn't introduced him as the Glassmaker when you arrived."

Unlike some unmated women more than twenty winters old, Ophelia had never been pressured by her parents to join her life with another's. So, hearing her mother speak of Rylan's physical appearance and outspoken demeanor, with approval, was foreign to her. Ophelia didn't dwell on it; she simply continued to brush her hair and allowed her mother to talk.

It wasn't as if she was speaking on him unfairly. Rylan was bold—more like direct. He was also very...virile in his physical appearance. If that was even a way to describe a being such as him. Just as tall as her brothers, he was broad across the shoulders and chest. The way his arms flexed as he worked the tools to shape the glass while he read the sparks held her entranced.

Initially, she'd attributed her intense focus to her anticipation of actually having a Glassmaker declare her blessing. However, when she'd watched him perform the tasks again for the little boy, Ophelia realized it wasn't simply because she'd been anxious to hear of her own gift. It was him. The confidence in his movements—no matter what the task—was mesmerizing.

Places inside her that she'd ignored awakened. Only now, as she sat listening to her mother, could she admit to herself it frightened her. It had from the moment Kieran told her she and Rylan shared mate ties. She'd determined she would live her life assisting her family in whatever way she could.

Everything had changed when she dismounted her steed and entered Rylan's workshop. One look at the larger-than-life Glassmaker in his protective leathers, and she'd never been the same. In a glance, she'd taken in his chestnut brown hair gathered in a haphazard arrangement atop his head; his large hands rested on his biceps as he'd watched them with his arms folded across his massive chest.

Rylan's sharp green eyes carried flecks of gold in their depths. The gold flecks she didn't notice until they sat together in his home. Her awareness of male beings had never been more keen. So wrapped in her remembrances, Ophelia didn't realize her mother had asked a question requiring a response. A physical nudge to her shoulder brought her back into the present.

"My apologies, Mama. What did you say?"

Clicking her tongue, her mother batted Ophelia's brush hand away and began to apply the hair cream to that section. She didn't repeat her question and the two worked in silence until Ophelia's hair was twisted and arranged atop her head. Regarding her reflection in the mirror, Ophelia thought the style was a mite intricate for normal activities, but she didn't complain.

The length and thickness of her hair made it a chore to handle on her best rotations. Having her mother's help cut the task in more than half. So, Ophelia would indulge her mother's penchant for eye catching hairstyles if it meant she didn't have to do it herself.

"Now that we're done, maybe you can listen to me without drifting off into your thoughts."

Hearing the serious notes in her mother's voice, Ophelia turned on the bench. Her mother patted the space next to her on the settee placed at the foot of the bed. Obediently, Ophelia joined her. As soon as she was seated, her mother clasped one of her hands.

"You've had a great deal of information thrust onto you in a short amount of time. And, while my heart is filled with joy in having confirmation that you are the fulfillment of the Enchantress's prophecy, I can also recognize the weight of such a blessing.

When you left home, I got the feeling you thought this journey would end like all the others. Did you think since your papa and I didn't come with you that we'd lost faith? We didn't. We decided your brothers were sufficient protection while we stayed here to look after everyone else. So, talk to me, Phely. How are you fairing?"

Ophelia searched her mind for the correct words to explain her whirling thoughts to her mother. It was hard to determine where to start, because her mother's intuition was correct. Damien had even given it voice before he approached Rylan. If she'd been unable to receive her blessing at Thistledown, there would not be another attempt made.

They would have to accept she was indeed among the unblessed. It wasn't a curse to not receive an extraordinary gift. She wouldn't be condemned to a terrible life because of it. In the nearly thirty winters she'd lived after her first visit to the Glassmaker, her only times of stress had centered around those visits.

In her daily life, she'd never been concerned at her inability to move the earth like her cousin or heal people with a touch like her mother. Ophelia didn't covet any of the blessings her brothers and those around her possessed.

"I guess I am fairing as well as can be expected, Mama. I know nothing about being Ergokin. How it works. How to control it. How it even feels when the blessing is active. What if I have been using it without conscious thought, and unknowingly causing harm?"

The combination of being able to speak her truth and her mother's compassionate response, led Ophelia to retelling the events from the time she'd met Rylan until the moment they arrived home. Recounting the sensation of somehow touching and amplifying Ramo's blessing to keep them hidden brought the emotions of the moment back to the surface.

With her mother, Ophelia was able to process the things she hadn't been able to give a voice to. She was also able to understand, just as she couldn't run from her extraordinary blessing, she couldn't pretend her connection to Rylan didn't exist.

She was able to somewhat resolve in her mind, what her instinct had been trying to tell her for the past four rotations. The Glassmaker was her life mate. To pretend she did not share the connection with him was fruitless.

The two women talked until they were summoned to rejoin the males in the main hall. Butterflies took flight in Ophelia's tummy as she considered seeing Rylan again with her recently accepted knowledge. Linking arms with her mother, she tilted her chin, determined to face whatever came next head on.

Chapter Thirteen

Rylan stood before the hearth with his back to the door. No fire blazed there. So, no warmth could be gathered. It didn't stop him from staring into the depths, tracing the patterns of previous flames in the burn marks on the stones.

Picking up the sound of soft footfalls, he turned toward the entrance. However, he didn't move until Ophelia actually entered the room. Confusion creased her brow, but she continued to walk closer to him.

"Where is everyone?" Her eyes darted around the space which was obviously devoid of other beings.

It had taken more convincing than he liked, but less than he expected, to persuade them to allow him to be alone with her to discuss their future. Approaching her slowly, he clasped her hand in his leading her to sit.

Her fresh scent assailed him. He wasn't sure if he should thank the goddess for whoever created the bath oils, or curse them for enhancing her natural aroma to such distracting levels. The urge to bury his nose in her neck and nip at her skin was nearly overwhelming. Her bewildered expression kept him from acting on the impulse. First, they must talk.

Then, if the goddess was on his side, they'd have no more than a night separating them before they could join.

"I asked them for time alone with you." Capturing both of her hands in his, he gently squeezed her digits trying not to be sidetracked by the smoothness of her skin.

"Why do we need to be alone, Rylan?"

Stroking the backs of her hands, he peered into her eyes.

"I know you didn't want to leave earlier. And, there are things that should be said which I would prefer remain between the two of us."

A nod was her only reply. Holding him captive with her golden gaze, she regarded him expectantly. So lost in their depths, it took him a moment to understand she was waiting for him to begin their discourse. It was logical, as he was the one who initiated the conversation.

"Sweeting, has your father ever told you the tale of the Leanders and the Firefists?"

When her eyes flicked to the tapestry on the wall, he knew she'd at least been told something.

"Yes. There is a blood feud between our families. It's because of them that the Leanders are in Misthaven and not Willowmere, our ancestral home."

"So, you are aware of the reasons your family believe you to be the one the Enchantress prophesied? The one who will restore honor to the Leander line?"

Ophelia narrowed her eyes. And, for the first time, her fingers gripped his.

"Why do I feel there is more to the story than what I know? They never really told me how our family's honor was lost—only that it was and the Firefists were involved."

Rylan didn't care for the look of betrayal etched across her beautiful face, but he wouldn't withhold anything—especially when it directly concerned her. So, he recounted his conversation with her father and his retelling of the origin of the feud between the Leanders and the Firefists. When he was done, he silently watched her filter through the information.

He considered if she'd come to the same possible conclusion he had. Rylan hadn't breathed a word to her father and brothers about another possible meaning of the prophecy. Since such things could be interpreted a myriad of ways, it was likely the possibility had occurred to someone and been dismissed due to the state of the family's reputation.

"I've always wondered in what way my blessing would return honor to my family."

Her fingers gripped his as she looked at him with a mixture of confusion and clarity in the golden depths of her eyes. Rylan didn't have a lengthy wait to learn what she'd determined.

"Could it be that they think my blessing would be so attractive we could reconcile with the Firefists through a mating? Does my father expect me to mate with some stranger to restore the family name? Are there even any male heirs in the Firefist line?"

Cradling her face in his hands, Rylan shushed Ophelia before she could work herself into a state. It felt like the most natural thing in the world to press his lips to hers in a chaste kiss.

"Shh... Sweeting. You won't be forced to mate with a stranger." Pulling back, he looked into her eyes once more. "Unless you still consider *me* to be a stranger."

Ophelia's eyes widened revealing the green flecks in their amber depths. Her jaw dropped, but no sound escaped her mouth. Rylan wasn't sure if he should interpret her stunned expression as encouragement or a deterrent.

"Sweeting, why are you surprised? Did I not express my desire to be your mate earlier? Or did you expect your father to turn me away?"

When she finally spoke, her voice held a breathy quality as

if the words were drifting along the air passing through her lips.

"I wasn't sure what I expected."

Unable to resist, Rylan pressed another kiss to her lips before placing one on her forehead.

"You didn't tell me your brother Kieran was a Soulkin." At the mention of her brother, Ophelia's eyelids closed briefly before she lifted them again.

"So, you know."

"Yes, Sweeting. I know. But it wouldn't have mattered. What he said was simply confirmation of what I felt the moment I saw you."

Ophelia's soft hands wrapped around his wrists as far as they could reach, and Rylan allowed her to tug his hands from her face. Unwilling to completely break the connection, he clasped her fingers with his, resting them on his thigh. Searching her face, he tried to discern what she was thinking.

"What is it, Sweeting?"

"I've never so much as been courted, Rylan." Her fingers rotated beneath his and she tangled their digits together. "Just now, when you pressed your lips to mine, it was the first time I'd been kissed by a male."

Rylan inhaled sharply. Her innocence wasn't a requirement, but hearing of it had an unanticipated effect. He became even more determined to have them be joined as mates. The knowledge that he was the first and would be the only male to experience her sweetness had moisture gathering in his mouth in keenness to partake in her feminine delicacy.

Not wanting to frighten her, he gathered himself before responding. He'd sensed some hesitancy on her part, but had attributed it to her being cautious in the company of an unknown male. His newly acquired knowledge allowed him to understand her previous behavior hadn't been completely a result of conforming to propriety as an unmated female.

"You honor me, Sweeting." Rubbing his thumb along her hand, he probed her with his stare. "I won't pretend I'm not eager to have us joined together, but know that my readiness doesn't come before your needs."

Releasing one hand, he cupped the side of her face. Stroking her cheek, he searched her eyes for answers. Initially, he'd thought the amber pools were identical to her brothers and their father. However, now, he saw something different in Ophelia's. A male could nearly drown in their pure depths.

"Sweeting, it would be wonderful if there was time for me to court you properly. I will admit, I don't know a great deal about the practice. However, for you, I would try."

Kissing her forehead, he drew back recapturing her gaze. "We both know time isn't our ally. With what we've learned from your father and what happened on the road, getting to the Keeper is imperative. But, I don't want to leave this place the same as I came. I want to be joined with you. To officially be your mate. We have the confirmation of a respected Soulkin. So, there is no doubt we are meant for each other."

Chapter Fourteen

Following Rylan's declaration, Ophelia could barely hear anything over the thundering of her heart. Her thoughts were whirling causing her to feel light headed. Had it not been less than six rotations since they'd met? It had. She was certain of it. Yet this male sat with her in her family home proclaiming his desire to be joined with her as mates. ***Mates!***

A stillness came over her as she attempted to understand how her life had changed so quickly. This was ***not*** how she'd seen things occurring. She was to be a forever aunt, helping her brothers with their younglings and caring for their parents as they aged. Now. This male. This Glassmaker...was suggesting she toss all of that aside. To bind her life to his.

Gently, but firmly, she withdrew her hands from his. Standing, she blocked the twinge of guilt she felt for pulling away. His disappointment in her withdrawal from him was plainly displayed on his features. She hadn't intended it as a rejection. Ophelia simply needed physical space to think.

Unfortunately, space was a luxury she could only enjoy for a few scant sands. She was barely three steps away from Rylan when a cacophony of sounds reached her ears. High, gleeful voices proceeded the appearance of two little girls and a smaller boy. Her brother Jaime's younglings.

"Chee-Chee!" The little brown bundles of energy barreled into the room, racing toward Ophelia.

Genuinely happy to see them, she dropped into a crouch ready to catch the first small person to fling themselves into her arms. Hugs and kisses were the order of business for the next several minutes as the younglings chattered—each attempting to fill her in on the important happenings she'd missed. Ophelia soaked it up while dodging questions about where she'd been and why she'd been gone so long.

All chatter came to an abrupt halt when Elysia asked a question which stole Ophelia's ability to speak. The oldest of Jaime's three offspring, her niece was inquisitive and had always been encouraged to ask for answers when she wanted to learn something. Ophelia now regretted supporting such behavior.

"Chee-Chee, is he your mate? Papa said you have a mate, and we'd get to attend the binding ceremony today."

Instead of answering Elysia, Ophelia looked to her second oldest brother. Even beneath his chestnut brown complexion, she detected the additional color in his face. Movement to his left drew her attention to the others now gathered in the room. All of whom wore similar expressions. It dawned on Ophelia that everyone, including Rylan had freshened and changed. They no longer carried the dust of the road on their garments.

Gathering herself, Ophelia returned her gaze to Elysia. Tapping the tip of her niece's button nose, she smiled at the little girl.

"Why don't you take your brother and sister to the garden to play while I talk to the other grown-ups?"

Not to be deterred, Elysia asked again. Skillfully dodging and redirecting, Ophelia didn't respond with any real answers.

When one of the caretakers led them from the room, Ophelia whirled on her family with fire blazing in her eyes. However, before she could light into anyone, Rylan was standing before her.

His large hands cupped her shoulders as he leaned in until everyone, who wasn't him, was obscured from her vision.

"Sweeting, I thought we had longer to discuss it. But it appears the sands have run out. So, I require your answer now. Will you join with me? Bind our lives together? Be my mate?"

Warmth spread from where Rylan's hands rested on her shoulders up to her face, heating her cheeks. The weight of his question and his penetrating stare added to the urgency of the moment. Ophelia's vocal cords failed her and all she could muster was a dazed nod. Apparently, that small acknowledgement was enough to catapult the household into a flurry of activity.

Two turns of the hourglass later, Ophelia stood in the garden where she'd tried to send her niece to play. The lush foliage was the perfect backdrop for a binding ceremony. The arched trellis overflowing with colorful blossoms was the same one used for each of her mated brothers' ceremonies as well as many others living on Leander lands. As the patriarch, her father would lead them in the ritual.

Keeping the tremble from her hands was as impossible as convincing herself she wasn't standing before all of her loved ones getting ready to pledge her life to the ruggedly handsome Glassmaker she'd known for less than a quarter of a moon cycle. Rylan's long, thick fingers clasped hers in a steady hold. Lifting her eyes from their joined digits, Ophelia found his waiting for hers. The caring and warmth he projected eased her nervousness, calming her fearful tremors.

She wasn't afraid of Rylan. For reasons only known to the goddess, she'd never feared the large male. It was the unknown wrapped in the unexpected causing her anxiety. She'd begun the rotation as an unmated female of thirty-four Winters. It would end with her life being bound to the male who'd read the sparks and pronounced her blessing.

Her father stood before them, holding a long golden cord. The diameter of the corded thread was comparable to Ophelia's fingers—or slightly thicker. It was only when he spoke that was she able to tear her gaze away from Rylan's.

"On this rotation, before our families, we petition the goddess to bless the mating of Rylan of the Sunweavers of Thistledown to Ophelia of the Leanders of Misthaven."

Lifting their joined hands, he began wrapping the cord around their linked digits. Starting at Rylan's wrist, he wound the golden rope until he reached the same area on her wrist. Once he was done, he enclosed their hands with both of his— one on top and the other below.

"Let this cord serve as a symbol of your bond to one another. May the ties of your union inextricably link you together. May your connection be so strong, no living being could penetrate it to unravel the thread."

Pausing, her father pierced Rylan with an expression containing equal parts warning, censure and approval.

"Rylan, Ophelia is now in your care. It is now your honor, privilege and duty to provide for her in all the ways a male should care for his female. Do you accept this charge?"

"I accept." Rylan's gruff voice was even deeper, scraping over Ophelia's skin as he made his pledge.

"Ophelia, Rylan is now in your care. It is now your honor, privilege and duty to provide for him in all the ways a female should care for her male. Do you accept this charge?"

Despite her trepidation, the words left her lips clearly. Maybe slightly breathier than her normal tone, but clear nonetheless.

"I accept."

"As this cord binds you together, let it serve has a proclamation of the unseen thread tethering your two souls together. May the goddess smile upon you for the rest of your rotations. Rylan, you may salute your mate."

Ophelia's eyes widened as Rylan lowered his head. Using the binding tying them together, he tugged her closer until his lips connected with hers. Her eyelids drifted closed and she was caught up in the feeling of his lips on hers. A startled gasp caused her lips to separate when his tongue swiped across them. His foray inside her mouth was brief, but enough to set off a different fire inside Ophelia—one she wasn't certain she wanted extinguished.

In a slight daze, Ophelia opened her eyes. Amber clashed with green with Rylan still being so close to her following their kiss. Once again, her father's voice was the only thing pulling her attention away. As he spoke, he released the cord binding their hands together.

"As I remove the physical tie binding you together, I encourage you to remember what it represents. Do not forget the unseen thread tying you together from now into eternity."

The moment their hands were freed, a cheer went up in the garden. Surprised, Ophelia turned to see her mother, along with her brothers' mates, clapping and exclaiming their joy. Her mother swiped at wetness on her cheeks while wearing the largest smile Ophelia had ever seen grace her beautiful face.

Everything felt unreal and too tangible simultaneously. What now? She had only her limited view of her parents mating as her example. How was she to proceed? Rylan answered at least one of her questions when he slipped one arm around her waist and anchored her to his side. His claim was clear.

Only the tiny hands of the littles were able to persuade him to release his hold. Elysia held onto one of her legs while Lillian commandeered the other—leaving Orion without a place to land. His chin jutted forward as he considered his options. Looking to Rylan, he lifted his arms and demanded, "Up!"

It may as well have been a command from the head of the queen's guard instead of the high-pitched voice of a small youngling. Rylan smoothly scooped Orion into one arm and the boy promptly began to explore Rylan's beard. Watching them together, Ophelia's stomach clenched in yet another unfamiliar feeling. She couldn't prevent herself from imagining what he would be like with their own offspring. Which led her to wonder about their immediate future following their joining.

Chapter Fifteen

Rylan's chest was filled with emotions he was in no way acquainted with. This rotation had proven to be auspicious from its very start. After hearing the story of the Leanders, he'd been skeptical regarding whether her father would accept his mate claim to Ophelia. When the opportunity had arisen for them to be officially joined, he'd jumped at the chance.

It was understood amongst them that time was of the essence and they would have to soon leave Leander lands to make the journey to the Keeper. Rylan was not keen on traveling another rotation unable to touch or be closer than an arm's length to Ophelia. Still, he was certain the swiftness was overwhelming to her.

When he secured some alone time with her, part of what he was supposed to do was speak to her about the ceremony. However, to him, his first duty was to share with her the other discussion held between the males. He simply misjudged how long relaying such information would take, leading them to their current situation.

Ophelia was handling it well, but he felt the tremors in her hands before the ceremony and the slight uncertainty in her movements and responses once it was done. Somehow, the Leanders had pulled together a celebratory meal fit for royalty in a short span. If he appeared to be a male obsessed with his mate, Rylan didn't care. He couldn't stop staring at Ophelia or touching her in some small way.

Even the younglings taking turns climbing on the two of them didn't stop him. The littles were eventually ordered to their own seats near their parents, but their presence didn't deter Rylan. If he were a different male, he would've felt some shame at his eagerness to put an end to the celebration so that he could take Ophelia to her rooms.

His hunger to join with her in the ways of a mated couple was larger than what he felt for the savory dishes placed before him on the table. The sweet fruit his mate suggested he consume for dessert only made him imagine if her nectar would hold the same saccharine flavor.

"Are you okay, Sweeting?"

Rylan's gaze tracked Ophelia as she strolled farther into the outer sitting area in her set of rooms. Her arms were folded across her middle and her posture was erect. Too erect. Too formal. When she stopped pacing and turned toward him, her amber eyes told him everything he needed to know.

Remembering her earlier confession regarding her experience with males, he didn't approach her. Instead, he sat on the tufted divan. Watching her for a few beats, he tapped the empty space next to him with an open palm.

"Come, Sweeting. Sit. We should talk."

Ophelia's steps were slow, but she didn't reject his request. Although calling it a request was generous. He waited until she was seated before he questioned her again.

"Sweeting, are you okay?"

"Yes...No...Possibly?"

Smiling at her honest confusion, Rylan adjusted himself slightly closer and wrapped an arm around her shoulder. Tugging her until she leaned on his chest, he stroked her back and arm in an attempt to reassure her.

"Sweeting, much has happened very quickly. It's normal if you're not fine."

Leaning against the high back of the furniture he ignored the thudding of his heart and the feelings of lust lingering beneath the surface. She didn't need him seeking to rut her at the first opportunity. They were mated. They had infinite rotations ahead of them in which to indulge in carnal delights.

"What happens now?" Ophelia's words were slightly muffled against his chest.

"Whatever we want to happen will happen next. This night begins the rest of our rotations together in this realm. We will need to leave here soon to go to the Keeper."

Ophelia shifted until her chin was resting against his chest as she stared into his eyes.

"How soon?"

"No more than three rotations. I don't believe Caspian will give up simply because his mercenaries weren't able to get to you on the journey here. I'm certain they've returned to him by now. We want to be on our way before they're able to determine where you're from."

A line appeared in the center of Ophelia's brow. "He would be bold enough to venture onto Leander lands?"

Cupping her face, Rylan rubbed the silk of her cheek before placing a gentle kiss on her forehead.

"Sweeting, we should never put limits on what the greedy will do in their attempt to gain more. The first effort didn't end as anticipated. So, he will likely adjust and try an alternate approach.

If it were me, I'd ask around about the family in the village before venturing further. But, Caspian isn't known for his patience."

Rylan made a notation to himself to discuss the possibility with the Leander males. They should have someone in the village watching for the arrival of strangers asking questions. Having committed that thought to memory, he returned to his task of soothing his mate.

They both would have to make adjustments, but he appeared to be the only one of them looking forward to the prospect. Although, in fairness, his eagerness to physically join with her contributed to his anticipation.

"Enough about Caspian for now. We are here together. And you are safe."

Rylan tightened his embrace. He released a chuff of contentment when Ophelia snuggled into him with her head on his chest. Her allowing him this degree of intimacy thrilled him. Although holding her in his arms and smelling her alluring scent was a form of torture, he reveled in the quiet moment with his mate.

Without his consent, his maleness swelled in his trousers. It was only because he hadn't fully arranged her on his lap that she didn't feel it as well. Lazily, he stroked along her arm with his fingertips. He was enamored with her silky skin. The brown tone resembled the color of rich earth. *Fertile* earth. Having thoughts of fertility while in proximity to Ophelia's lush body was likely not the best idea.

Rylan stiffened in an effort to remain still and refrain from tugging on his own shaft to get relief. That would be a terrible introduction to coupling for his innocent mate. Despite his best efforts, Ophelia noticed his discomfort.

"Rylan?" Once again peering into his face, Ophelia finished her query without words.

"It's nothing, Sweeting." Rylan caressed her shoulder as he shook his head.

Heat radiated from the hand she placed on his chest and Rylan nearly groaned from the innocuous contact. Until then, her hands had been clasped together primly in her lap. Having them on him, even through the barrier of his shirt was havoc on his senses. When her deft fingers traveled from his chest to his beard, he nearly lost his control.

"I know it's something, Rylan. Your body. It feels...Different. Like you're uncomfortable. Should I move?"

When Ophelia shifted to follow through with her suggestion, Rylan quickly stilled her motion.

"That isn't necessary, Sweeting. You are perfect precisely where you are."

Even if having her so close and doing nothing but holding her was torture, it was torture Rylan would gladly endure to keep her close.

"Are you certain?"

The tender confusion in her expression made it impossible for him to resist pressing another kiss to her forehead. Ophelia released a light giggle, ducking her head and burrowing into his chest.

"Your beard tickled my nose." She explained as she cuddled against him once more.

"That is not the only place it will tickle."

Rylan could not have prevented the words from issuing forth given his best effort. Ophelia's giggles came to a swift end with a sharp inhale. Hugging her to his chest, he chastised himself for the looseness of his tongue.

"My apologies, Sweeting. I do not seek to scandalize you."

Looking up at him shyly, she plucked at the rounded collar of his shirt. Silence reigned for a few moments before she spoke.

"I'm not a youngling, Rylan. You don't have to tiptoe around me on kitten paws."

"Believe me, Sweeting. No one is more aware than I that

you are not a youngling. I simply didn't want to make you feel as if I am only capable of thinking carnal thoughts."

Him being almost completely consumed with carnal thoughts at the moment was inconsequential. At least to him. Rylan observed the flush creeping into the apples of Ophelia's cheeks. She was magnificent, and he was the most fortunate male in the realm to have her as his mate.

"Aren't mates supposed to think such thoughts about each other? There is no shame in it. Is it?"

Staring into her eyes, Rylan saw her sincerity. Her posture held a hint of wariness, but her chin tilted up in a show of bravery. His sweet mate was determined to address their issues head on. With his lips stretching into an uncharacteristic smile, he lifted her hand from his chest, brought it to his lips and kissed each digit individually.

"You are correct, Sweeting. There is no shame in having carnal thoughts about one's mate."

Her lashes lowered, hiding her amber pools from him before lifting and pinning him with an expression he couldn't quite read.

"Can you tell me about them?" Her voice was low, slightly husky and tinged with what sounded to Rylan's ear like desire.

"Can I tell you about my thoughts?"

"Yes."

"Absolutely, my sweet mate." Rylan didn't disguise the gruff need in his words.

Chapter Sixteen

Ophelia shifted her gaze from Rylan's eyes to his lips. When he'd smiled, her insides did a little flip inspiring her to squeeze her legs together. She'd never in her many rotations been so forward with a male. But, Rylan was *her* mate. If she couldn't give voice to her thoughts with him, who could she do it with?

A flash of pink appeared when Rylan swiped his tongue across his lips before he granted her request. The brief talk her mother had given her before the binding ritual was a jumble in her mind. But, one key piece of advice resonated with Ophelia.

*"Your mate may be large and gruff in his appearance, but he will never hurt you. I can see it in the way he looks at you and the way he seeks your comfort in all things. So, there is no need for you to fear what happens between you. You have simply to ask and he **will** do whatever is necessary to grant your wish. Use that knowledge to make certain your first joining and any thereafter are pleasing for both of you."*

Having her mother discuss intimate things with her after so many winters could've been embarrassing, but the swiftness of events didn't lend themselves toward such indulgences. As she waited for Rylan to grant her request, she endeavored to maintain her bold façade. Only when he began to speak did the pretense slip.

"First... I was thinking of how I enjoy the feel of your skin."

As he spoke, Rylan traced random patterns on her arms. The lightly calloused tips of his fingers scraped gently over her skin, leaving tingles in their wake. The warmth building in Ophelia's center shifted to a low pulsation under his touch. When he confessed that her brown skin reminded him of fertile earth, the pulsing became more insistent.

"Then, when you mentioned being tickled by my beard, I thought of how delightful it would be to tickle the valley between your thighs with my whiskers as I feasted on your sweet nectar."

Ophelia's breath hitched at the mention of him placing his mouth near her untouched mons. Instead of shocking her, his words intrigued her.

"How..." Clearing the uncertainty from her throat, Ophelia tried again. "How does a male...feast on a female's nectar?"

Despite the certainty that she shouldn't be ashamed to ask her mate such questions, Ophelia didn't look Rylan in the eyes when she asked.

"Would you like me to show you, Sweeting?"

The deep timbre and promise in his voice reached inside her and squeezed Ophelia in her intimate places. Even without experiencing it before, she recognized the lustful feeling. Finally returning her stare to her mate's hypnotic green eyes, she nodded in response.

"I must hear you say the words, Sweeting. Would you like me to show you how a male feasts on the nectar from his female's puss?"

Unbidden, Ophelia's lips parted. Her "yes" escaped on a breeze passing through them. A mercurial transformation occurred in Rylan immediately. A sensual darkness descended over his features.

Closing the scant distance between them, Rylan tugged her to him by her nape and pressed his lips to hers. Unlike the relatively chaste kiss he'd given her during their ceremony, he used his tongue to coax her lips apart. Delving inside, he persuaded her tongue to dance with his. A moan bubbled in Ophelia's throat from the decadent feel of her first real kiss.

It felt amazing. Although…it wasn't what she expected. Rylan scattered her thoughts when the hand not cradling her head grazed across her breasts. The zing which accompanied the light touch made her breath catch in her throat. Giving her life breaths, her mate continued introducing her to new pleasures.

Cupping one breast, he squeezed it causing the nipple hiding beneath the fabric of her dress to pucker with want. *Want for what though?* Ophelia's silent question was answered when Rylan's nimble fingers released the stringed bow holding the two sides of her bodice together. The heat gliding beneath her skin increased when his roughened fingertips caressed her now exposed mounds.

"Oh!" The feeling was so pleasurably foreign, she couldn't stop herself from crying out.

"Do you like that, Sweeting? The feel of my hands on your ripe melons. Do you want me to worship them as well?"

The delightful sensations inspired by his touch were increased by the promise in his queries. Did she want those things? *Goddess yes*! But how did she express her desire? She had little to no control of herself under his sensual onslaught.

"It's okay, my sweet mate. I know what you need."

Rylan followed his declaration by standing from the divan and lifting her in his arms. The weightless feeling was quickly replaced by awe at how amazing it felt being held in his embrace. Braced against his broad chest, Ophelia was emboldened to tilt her face to his to resume the connection of their lips. It was only when her back met soft bed coverings that she realized he'd brought them to her bedchamber.

"Sweeting, we must rid you of this dress."

Rylan's heavy voice matched the darkness in his eyes. Ophelia offered no objection to him peeling the flowing gown from her body. Her desire to experience all which occurred between mates didn't give her room to be shy. The cool air wafting across her newly exposed skin wasn't the cause of the goose pimples rising on her arms.

No. It was the fire in her mate's eyes when he gazed upon her naked form. He looked as if he wanted to devour her. Instead of her wanting to hide her feminine parts from his scrutiny, Ophelia felt powerful. This large, handsome male was entranced from simply looking at her bare. Wetness gathered in her feminine folds from him simply watching her. Once he actually touched her, Ophelia thought she might jump from her skin. *Were intimate relations between mates supposed to feel like this?*

Using kisses, Rylan clouded her already jumbled thoughts. With her back once again meeting the soft bed coverings, Ophelia latched on to his thick tresses when he began kissing a trail down her neck. Stopping at her breasts, he lavished attention on her turgid peaks nearly sending her flying into the unknown with pleasure.

True to his earlier statement, his beard tickled her skin in each place he kissed. Though, her response to the new sensation wasn't a giggle as it was before. Instead, her skin pebbled in the wake of his amorous attention.

Ophelia's eyes widened and her lips formed a perfect 'O' when Rylan's roughened digits touched the insides of her thighs, opening her legs and creating space for his wide shoulders. Her fingers flexed in his hair releasing the long strands from the now disheveled top knot he'd worn for their binding ceremony. The hungry expression on his face would have one thinking he hadn't gotten his fill during dinner earlier.

She hadn't imagined herself mating with anyone, so Ophelia had no expectation of how coupling was supposed to occur. However, Rylan's intensity set off tremors inside her. At the first touch of his lips to her folds, he stole her breath. When he ran a finger between them opening her flower for his complete devouring, Ophelia thought she'd perish from the lustful feelings washing over her.

It was after he latched onto her secret place with a suckling kiss that she completely lost her connection to reality. A keening moan tore from Ophelia's throat and her back arched. Control wasn't a consideration as her hips bucked trying to get closer to the source of the mind-blowing pleasure. Rylan's mouth. Adding to her heightened awareness, he groaned sending vibrations through her center.

Ophelia's eyes slammed shut. Stars bloomed behind her eyelids as her core clenched and her body jerked with her release. As any female coming of age had done, Ophelia had explored her body. But, nothing prepared her for Rylan's mastery with his tongue. He hadn't even used his fingers as she had done during her own explorations.

"Your nectar is even sweeter than I thought it would be."

Rylan's breath on her sensitive mons sent another tremor through Ophelia's body. Still unable to form words, a gasping whimper accompanied her quivers. Opening her eyes, Ophelia watched as Rylan placed a kiss on her petals then rose to his knees between her spread legs.

Her eyes widened in shock at the image he presented. She had no recollection of him removing his garments, but his chest was bare displaying the dusting of dark hair lightly covering his rippling muscles in a trail leading down his torso into his trousers. *Oh, my goddess, he was beautiful.*

"Thank you, Sweeting. But I believe you are the true beauty in this mating."

Ophelia's embarrassment at speaking her internal thoughts aloud was squelched when Rylan removed the last of his garments revealing his maleness. The length and thickness of his shaft shifted her thoughts completely to what would be expected of her next.

Chapter Seventeen

Rylan watched Ophelia visually exploring his body. Ignoring the demands of his aching cock. He allowed her to study him —to get comfortable with his naked form.

"You can touch me as well, Sweeting. I am yours."

His breath locked in his chest when her soft palm landed on his midsection, mere inches from his aching maleness. The organ in question twitched in anticipation, drawing a squeak from his mate and a quick withdrawal. Keeping his features neutral, Rylan remained completely still as she built up her courage and made a second attempt. This time, she went directly for his throbbing shaft.

"Goddess…"

The word was drawn out to the point of singing, but Rylan didn't care. He felt as untried as his mate when he nearly spilled his seed from the slight contact. A drop of his essence pearled at the tip of his stiffness, and he nearly folded in half when Ophelia leaned forward and licked it away.

Apologizing profusely, Rylan pulled her away from his engorged length. If her innocent touch had him on the verge of release, he couldn't allow her to put her mouth on him. Kissing away Ophelia's pout at having her exploration cut short, he settled his hips between her lush thighs.

"Sweeting, I'm going to fuck you now." Ophelia's pout disappeared and a hint of trepidation coated her expression.

Gently kissing her plush lips, Rylan aligned himself with her sweet puss and pressed forward notching the head of his shaft in the entrance of her heated core. Gritting his teeth, he watched her for any signs of discomfort. Her breath hitched and her lower lip disappeared between her teeth.

Her walls rippled slightly at his intrusion, but he resolved not to pummel her flower, no matter how tempting it was. When she squirmed beneath him, swiveling her hips, Rylan clamped a hand to her side to still her movements.

Watching the place where he was invading her sweet puss, Rylan prayed to the goddess for the endurance he needed to control himself. His speech was gruff and stilted when he spoke.

"Please. Sweeting. Do not move. I do not wish to hurt you."

"But, *you're* not moving and I ache so much."

Rylan felt the fire in his eyes when he swung his gaze up to her face. Biting her lower lip, with her lashes low over her amber orbs, she was the perfect image of a wanton female. Inexperienced she may be, but his mate was lusty and she wanted his cock. He could deny her nothing—especially not something which would bring them both pleasure.

"Hold onto me, my sweet. I will take care of the ache for you."

Rylan was proud of the confidence in his voice—how soothing he sounded while his insides danced in jubilation. His lower back burned from restraining himself. Ophelia's blunt nails dug into his flank as he began to slide forward penetrating her tight walls. Unable to prevent them, his eyes left her face to capture the equally beautiful sight of her flower opening to accept him.

Her breath escaped in melodious tones as he continued to press forward past her maidenhead until he was seated completely inside her deliciously heated puss. Releasing his hold on her hip, Rylan brushed the disheveled coils of her hair away from her face. Dropping his forehead to hers, he pecked her lips coaxing them open for his invasion.

"Is this what you wanted, Sweeting?" Withdrawing his length halfway from her velvet channel, he slid back inside in a sure stroke.

"Did you want me to fuck you like this? Ravish you? Claim you in every way a male claims his female?"

Ophelia's lips parted, but only keening wails escaped. His sweet mate had lost her voice again. The knowledge swelled his length even more. Endeavoring to make her forget speech completely, Rylan dropped his head to the crook of her neck worrying the skin there as he increased the rhythm of his strokes.

Writhing beneath him, his mate matched his thrusts beautifully, bringing him even closer to spilling his seed inside her. When her pants became babbling, Rylan knew she was close to her completion. Thanking the goddess, he rose to his knees, and tilted her pelvis to meet his thrusts. Unerringly seeking her sensitive pearl, he rubbed it as he stroked his maleness into her channel.

"Rylan!"

Ophelia screamed his name. Her back was bowed leaving only her head and shoulders on the bed, and her walls convulsed around his length. Releasing his own shout of completion, Rylan let go. His lower half functioned on pure instinct. The pleasure of spilling his seed inside his mate was so intense it was as if he'd been lifted from this realm.

Dropping forward, he blanketed her body with his,

breathing heavily and peppering kisses on her face and neck. He had no idea he was capable of the sweet endearments he whispered in Ophelia's ears, praising her for how well she accepted his claim.

Not desiring to smother his new mate, Rylan eventually shifted to one side. Unable to lose contact with her completely, he curled his body around hers, tucking her delectable posterior into his groin. His deflated member twitched, but didn't stiffen. It was just as well. Considering the lustiness of their first coupling, his sweet mate and her spellbinding puss would require a moment or two of rest.

With that thought in mind, Rylan shifted. Ophelia's skin was reminiscent of silk beneath his lips when he pressed a kiss to her shoulder before leaving the bed. Her movements were slow, but Rylan noticed when she turned to watch him.

"Rylan?" Her love worn voice was a hoarse whisper.

"Shh, Sweeting. I will return shortly."

Rylan strode into the bathing chamber. The Leander's home boasted the convenience of water pulls—both hot and cold. So, he was able to prepare a bath without ringing for one of the servants to assist. As shy as his Sweeting behaved prior to their joining, he was certain she wouldn't want to announce to the household they'd officially consummated their union.

The flower scent which clung to his mate's skin filled the chamber as he tipped the small bottle of fragrant oil into the heated tub of water. For good measure, he tossed in some of the petals he spied in a nearby wooden bowl. Once everything was set to his satisfaction, Rylan went into the bedchamber to retrieve Ophelia.

Lying on her side facing the open entryway, her appearance was ethereal or fae-like in her slumber. He lamented having to wake her, but knew she would appreciate the warm bath. Gently lifting her into his arms, Rylan took her into the bathing room. Her eyes fluttered open, but closed almost as quickly when she snuggled into his chest, releasing a contented sigh.

Grateful, the bathtub was large enough to accommodate them both, he stepped into the warm water and sat, keeping Ophelia in his lap. When the wetness touched her rounded bum, her eyes flew open and she stiffened in his embrace.

"What?!"

"Shh, Sweeting. I have you. You are safe." Rylan murmured other soothing words until Ophelia once again relaxed in his hold.

"You drew me a bath?" A confused frown knitted her brow as she stared at him.

The upper section of the porcelain, not covered by the warm water, felt cool against Rylan's back as his shoulder lifted in a shrug. Settling against him again, Ophelia began tracing the pattern of the markings on his chest and upper arm. Similarly, he ran his palm and fingertips along her body from her nape to the roundness of her plump posterior—lingering there briefly before moving upward once more.

"Is this what mates normally do after coupling?"

Although she continued to speak just above a whisper, a portion of her normal timbre had returned to her voice.

"As you are my first and only mate, I cannot say what is normal. Caring for you in this way is more of an instinct rather than a practiced routine I was taught to perform."

Rylan was uncertain if the warmth seeping inside him was from the liquid they rested in, having her plush body pressed against his, or the overall intimacy of being one with another being as he was with Ophelia. It didn't matter. While foreign, it was far from unpleasant. He'd remain as they were indefinitely if it were possible.

An internal pull in his groin preceded his shaft thickening.

The cause... his mate's lush bottom shifting against his length. Slick from the wetness surrounding them, her hips glided against the hands he placed on them to still her movements.

"Sweeting? What are you about? Your tender puss couldn't possibly take me again so soon."

Thick with barely checked desire, Rylan's words were strained. Twisting, Ophelia defied his restraint. Straddling him, with her knees resting alongside his thighs, she shifted their dynamic as well as position. Devouring her with his gaze, Rylan accepted her challenge—waiting for what she'd do next. She didn't leave him in suspense.

"Mate? Shouldn't I be the one of us who says whether I am capable of accepting your claim again? After all, the puss in question is attached to my body."

Her fingers clasping his length were soft against his hardness turning it to steel in her hold. Lust colored his gaze as he studied her movements. Displaying new confidence, his mate lowered herself onto his cock, sheathing him inside her velvet channel in excruciatingly slow increments. Rylan's fingers flexed against her hips, but he didn't assist her in her descent.

The sensual sounds she emitted were a decadent accompaniment to their coupling. When she began riding his cock like she was a skilled equestrian, and he was her prized steed, Rylan lost his battle to allow her complete control. Clamping his hands on her rounded arse, he guided her movements as he began thrusting his hips up to meet her downward motion.

Their coming together wasn't hurried, nor was it reserved. Neither appeared to be able to hold back from the other. Water sloshed around them as they ground their bodies together, not slowing until they were tossed over the cliff into their release. Rylan's teeth gnashed together at the clenching of his jaw.

Her walls pulsed around his turgid length as he spilled his

seed inside her once more. Ophelia's soft curls tickled his neck when she fell limply against his chest—spent from her first riding lesson.

Chapter Eighteen

The heat against her back differed from the warmth slanting across Ophelia's face. Opening her eyes, she quickly closed them in an attempt to block the brightness of the sun. The arm draped across her waist tightened, tugging her closer to the heat against her back. *Rylan*.

The events of the previous rotation and night flooded her mind with the recent memories. She was mated. They had consummated their union. Multiple times. The things her Glassmaker had taught her brought a different heat to her cheeks. Ophelia could only characterize her behavior as wanton. Even when he'd suggested they not continue to save her from discomfort, she couldn't seem to stop touching him and encouraging him to touch her.

Moisture pooled at her center, indicating the lustful thrall from her mating night hadn't lost its hold. The tickling scrape of Rylan's beard against her shoulder simply added to the desire building in her core. The female discussions with her mother didn't cover any of this. So, Ophelia had no understanding of if what she was experiencing was normal.

The roughened pads of Rylan's fingertips abraded her skin

when he clamped one hand at her hip. Until he'd applied pressure, halting her movements, she didn't know she was moving. Once she was forcibly stopped, she realized she'd been winding her bottom in circles seeking the hardness pressed against her.

"Stop, Sweeting. We must give care to your little flower."

The pout formed on her lips without Ophelia giving thought to putting it there.

"I thought we'd come to an agreement about you deciding what my puss could handle?"

As if she was lighter than a feather, Rylan shifted her body until she was on her back with him looming above her. His hair draped either side of his face in a dark wavy curtain, making her fingers itch to comb through it. His dark green eyes scanned her face before dropping to peruse the rest of her naked form. The heat of his stare elicited feelings as if he were touching her in every place his gaze landed.

With his eyes trained on her mound, he licked his lips.

"Let us compromise, Sweeting."

His statement was the only warning she received before he sank back on his knees, scooped her lower body up, and began lapping at her feminine folds. Until the rotation before, Ophelia had no idea couples engaged in such kissing. Now, she couldn't imagine a realm where it wasn't a requirement for mates to please one another in that manner. Tangling her fingers in the long brown strands, she held onto his head as he once again stoked the flame inside her.

Rylan's morning attention to her sensitive flower quickly took her over the edge into a trembling release. Vibrations from his moans shot through her quaking center. Uncaring of volume, she sang out her appreciation of her mate's skills. Pleasurable tingles skimmed over her skin as he placed gentle pecks to her puss. Spent and thoroughly relaxed, Ophelia's fingers loosened then dropped away from her hold on his hair.

Dropping her legs from his shoulders, Rylan kissed his

way up her body. Then, he gently took her mouth before pulling back to lie beside her once more. The bed shook slightly from his weight, jostling Ophelia closer to his side. Automatically, she curled into him with her head resting on his chest.

"Is that better for you, Sweeting?"

Ophelia had begun to drift back into dreamland when Rylan's question pulled her into awareness. Words weren't easily formed in her languid state. So, all she could manage was a sighing acknowledgement.

"Mhmm."

While she was ready to float back to sleep, her stomach had other ideas. Rumbling to announce its empty state, it drew a chuckle from Rylan.

"It appears I have sated one hunger only to awaken another."

Releasing a giggling sigh, Ophelia nestled closer into the warmth of his firm embrace. She was content to ignore the complaints of her belly. However, sturdy knocks to the outer door of her rooms pierced their happy bubble.

"Phely! Wake up! You and the Glassmaker are needed."

Two more hard knocks were delivered to the door before there was silence. By the time she and Rylan made it to the door, Damien was gone. Apparently, her oldest brother felt his message had been sufficiently delivered. Looking up at her new mate, Ophelia responded to the question in his expression.

"I don't know what it could be, but it must be important. Damien spends most mornings with his mate and their off-spring. It's only a few sands past first light."

Nodding in understanding, Rylan strode back into the bed chamber. "Then we must hurry to clothe ourselves and respond to the summons."

Rylan wouldn't get any arguments from her. Ophelia rushed through her cleanliness routine; then, she joined Rylan at the door. Blinking twice, she observed his change of clothing. So absorbed in her activities, she'd paid no attention to him moving around the space nor his satchel which was now clearly placed near the closed door.

"Are you anticipating leaving?"

Ophelia cleared her throat trying to remove the scratchy hitch which creeped in when she spoke. The prospect of him preparing to leave caused an unexpected swell of emotion that she couldn't keep out of her voice.

Following the direction of her stare, Rylan shook his head. His warmth enveloped her as he drew her closer to him. Without Ophelia stating her fears, he seemed to know what troubled her.

"I will not go from this place without you, Sweeting."

"Then, why...?" Her eyes once again sought out the bag next to the closed door.

"It is simply where it was placed when I brought it up yesterday."

Releasing a shaky breath, Ophelia nodded. Her movements were slightly jerky, but her uncertainty was eased by his explanation.

"Come. Let's go down before another of your brothers returns to beat the door down."

The dryness in his tone belied the upward tilt of his lips. The partial smile alerting her to his attempt at humor. Accepting his offered arm, she joined her mate in their trek downstairs.

Before they reached the entryway, Ophelia detected the low murmurs coming from the direction of the solarium. Tugging Rylan toward the sound, she strained her ears to pick up the conversational thread. She wanted to hear what they had to say prior to knowing the two of them were present. To her disappointment, nothing was audible enough for her to learn anything new.

The warmth of Rylan's fingers soothed her, as he lay his hand atop hers on his arm. Projecting reassurance, he led them into the room to join her family. Ophelia's gaze swept around the space. All of her brothers were present along with Damien's, Ramo's and Jaime's mates. Kieran was unmated, but it wasn't unusual for her brother's. None of them mated before they reached thirty and five Winters. So, he was only a year behind their schedule.

Her parents occupied one divan, her brother's mates the other, while her brothers stood around the hearth. Absent from the assembly were the younglings, but added to it were her cousin's mate, Magnus, along with Ronan. Ronan's presence was the most curious since he lived in the village, where he was the blacksmith. Although he'd been close friends with her brothers for many winters, he didn't make impromptu visits from Misthaven. If there was a planned activity such as a hunt, it was normal to see him about with the Leanders. Otherwise, Ophelia saw him primarily during their trips to the village.

The conversation in the room came to an abrupt halt when they entered moments before. Tiring of waiting for someone to speak, Ophelia looked to her parents expectantly.

"Mama, Papa, Damien said we were needed?"

Leading with the questioning tone, Ophelia tried to suppress her trepidation. She was immediately comforted by Rylan wrapping an arm around her waist. Without thought, she tucked into his side absorbing his warmth. His touch seemed to have a calming effect on her.

"Come sit, Ophelia." Her mother's soft command was issued with her extending a hand to the lover's bench on her left.

Obediently, Ophelia sat. Rylan chose to stand at her back with a hand on her shoulder. Leaning, she braced against him allowing his steadfastness to leak into her to maintain her composure.

"Phely, I wish there was more time..." Her mother trailed off, looking to her father. Draping an arm around his mate's shoulder, her father looked between Ophelia and Rylan.

"Ronan brought news from the village. There are strangers there asking questions. They didn't know names, but it didn't take much inquiry for them to learn of the family based on the descriptions they gave of the horses and colors worn by you and your brothers."

Ophelia's gaze immediately searched out Rylan's. His fingers tightened on her shoulder.

"Do you think the strangers were sent by Caspian?"

"If so, it means they didn't follow us directly. Otherwise, they would've been spotted on the road here instead of them going to the village."

Damien nodded in agreement with Rylan's assessment. "The males who tried to follow us could have doubled back when they lost our trail. It *has* been five rotations. If they rode hard, they could have returned to him and been sent out again to check in all the villages along the path to Misthaven."

Anxiety formed a ball in Ophelia's stomach. "What happens now? Do we wait before going to the Keeper?"

"No." Her father's voice was firm in his reply. "It is important for you to learn whatever you can about your blessing, and only the Keeper can truly guide you. But, before you go, we will have a formal gathering announcing your mating with the Glassmaker."

Damien stood up straight from his pose leaning against the hearth. "Are you sure that we should have a party, Papa? A large gathering would provide the strangers with an opportunity to get too close to Phely."

"They will *never* lay a hand on my mate." Rylan's already deep voice lowered with his growling response. Reaching up, Ophelia tangled her fingers with his on her shoulder.

Chapter Nineteen

The fire that erupted in Rylan's chest, when Damien suggested any being would come within touching distance of his Sweeting, was hot enough to ravage the Leander's vast fields. In order to ruffle one hair on Ophelia's lovely head, a body would have to end Rylan's existence. Such wouldn't be done without a considerable fight.

"Calm yourself, Glassmaker."

The elder Leander held up a hand to stem any further declarations from Rylan. He'd needn't have bothered. Rylan had said everything he intended. Additional explanation wasn't necessary.

"I have a plan. One which I hope will allow us to suss out their intentions, the intentions of their master and use the information to our benefit. If things go well, you will be in the Keeper's sanctuary before the scouts can report the wealth of misinformation they will receive at the celebration."

Ophelia's fingers flexed against his drawing his gaze to her upturned face. The sliver of fear he'd seen there earlier wasn't distinguishable. Her amber eyes searched his for confirmation of his agreement. Ophelia's waning fear was a testament to her trust in her father. However, he saw that she'd instinctively turned to him, her mate, to completely wipe away any lingering doubt.

Causing Ophelia distress wasn't what Rylan wanted. With a reassuring squeeze to her digits, he looked to her father once more.

"What is your plan?"

If Rylan had been impressed by their ability to put together a joining ceremony in less than a rotation, his head spun with the flurry of activity surrounding their formal mating celebration a mere two rotations later. It was during the preparations that he got to experience the varied blessings of the Leanders. It again made Rylan wonder about the elders' fixation on restoring the family honor.

At least three, possibly more, generations of Leanders inhabited the vast and lush property just outside of the village of Misthaven. They were almost a village unto themselves. He'd stood by staring in fascination as one of the females ran her fingers across an arch filled with shriveled twigs. In each place she touched, colorful blooms sprouted until the curved structure was overflowing with abundant flowers.

While his glassmaking skills weren't needed, Rylan was able to lend his muscle to the construction of a massive tented area to protect the revelers from the blazing sun. Since the celebration was set to begin in the early morning and go on throughout the rotation, shelter, aside from the main house, was required.

On the morning of their official mating celebration, Rylan was posted at the window in a chamber next to the one he shared with Ophelia, watching the distant carriages transporting well-wishers come closer. Some bore colorful banners, while others were more plain. But, they were numerous. They'd all come to see the Leander daughter and her Glassmaker mate.

The sight brought back the conversation he and Ophelia had the previous night. Lying in bed after a vigorous round of loving, with her head tucked beneath his chin, she absently traced the markings on his shoulder.

"Do you know why my papa is so certain there will be a large crowd here for the mating celebration?"

"Because your family is well respected in the area?"

Her fingers stilled briefly, before continuing to follow the swirling pattern on his skin.

"It's possible, but not the primary reason."

Something in her tone hinted at sadness. Rylan didn't like it. Tightening his hold on her, he rubbed her back in soothing circles. He didn't prompt her to continue, but he didn't have to.

"They want to see it for themselves. My papa's refusal to believe the first Glassmaker and those who followed is well known. Most don't know why he refused. The words of the Enchantress are a closely held family secret. But, my papa taking me to different Glassmakers across the realm...

That story is known by many. So, they want to meet you. They must see the male who's captured the hand of the unblessed daughter of the Leander patriarch. The daughter who was well past mating age. Only, we can't tell any of them the real truth of it. Can we?"

"No, Sweeting. We can't."

She was silent for so long Rylan would've thought she was sleeping. Except her fingers never stopped moving—and he could almost hear the thoughts turning in her head.

"Sweeting...What they think of you or who they thought you were doesn't matter. You have always had value. Being the mate of a Glassmaker. Having a rare and coveted blessing. Those are not the attributes which make you a being of great significance."

Tilting her face up, his stare probed her. "You are aware of this, right?"

The softness in her gaze was nearly Rylan's undoing. With a gentle smile, she nodded her agreement.

Pressing her head back onto his chest, he nuzzled the top of her massive curly coils. Placing a kiss on her forehead, he hugged her close.

"I suggest we get some rest, Sweeting. If your father's plan is successful, the next rotations will be very busy."

They'd drifted off to sleep only to be awakened by the first appearance of the big yellow ball in the sky—along with the knocks of the ladies who came to shoo him out of their bedchamber into the neighboring one. Amid the chaos, he was assured someone would come to attend him as well, but he had to leave so his mate could be made ready for the festivities.

True to their words, a couple of males came to assist him. Having packed his satchel with plain garments intended for travel, Rylan had nothing suitable for a celebration. It hadn't mattered during their mating ceremony. A clean shirt and breeches were all he required. Now, he considered the finery expected for such an occasion.

Ophelia's mother was a female of many talents beyond her blessing of healing. One of the males sent to attend him was a haberdasher. In very short order, he'd transformed Rylan. Upon inspection of himself in the looking glass, he admitted he barely recognized the male in the fitted hunter green breeches and coordinating gold tunic with green piping. Instead of flowing over his shoulders, he'd somewhat contained his hair in a more carefully constructed top knot than the one's he wore when he worked.

Turning away from the sight of their approaching guests,

Rylan left his temporary chamber. Although he longed to enter the rooms he shared with Ophelia, he continued on downstairs. He wanted one more chance to speak with Theron Leander before the festivities began. The elder was confident in his plan, but it wouldn't hurt to consider contingencies.

Unfortunately, or fortunately, depending on whose perspective was assumed, Rylan wasn't able to locate the other male. So, he returned to the upper floor to wait outside their chambers for his mate's exit. He didn't give thought to appearances. A promise had been made to his mate, and he intended to keep it. It meant, he wouldn't leave her side while strangers were about.

When the heavy wooden door opened, Rylan stood up straight from his position against the opposite wall. A contingent of females, including his mate's mother and the mates of Ophelia's brothers poured out of the room amid sighs and giggles. Each gave him a knowing glance in passing. Soft footfalls drew his attention back to the open doorway.

Ophelia was framed in the opening looking, to his eyes, like the queen of the fae. Devouring her with his gaze, Rylan stared at the vision of a being. The desire to make a special sacrifice to the goddess for his good fortune was strong.

His Sweeting's voluptuous figure was accentuated by a lace trimmed gown which cinched at the waist and flowed over her hips down to the tips of her toes. The color was an iridescent hue which changed depending on how the light struck it. It played off the golden glow of her eyes perfectly.

Her hair was mostly loose in springy coils about her shoulders. Tiny flowers were woven into small braids fanning outward from her beautiful face. Her already sun kissed brown skin seemed to glow even more brightly. The urge to march her back into their bed chamber was almost uncontrollable.

"Sweeting…" Rylan spoke the endearment in a husky breath which was foreign to his ears.

"Glassmaker." Ophelia tilted her head to the side as she assessed him. She'd spoken his craft as if it too were a term of endearment and not his task from the goddess.

Slow deliberate steps were taken to shrink the distance separating them. Although he feared his reaction to physically touching her, Rylan couldn't stop himself from doing just that. Her skin was silk beneath his fingertips as he cupped the side of her face. Tipping her chin upwards, he didn't resist the urge to press their lips together in the most chaste kiss he could manage. When they parted, Ophelia's eyes mirrored the desire in his own.

With another gentle peck to her plush lips, he pulled away. "Perhaps we should join the festivities below."

"Perhaps." She replied breathily.

Chapter Twenty

Ophelia had smiled so much, she thought her cheeks may seize in the position, locking her into the comical grin of a jester. It may have been worth it if they were joyful expressions. While many of the well-wishers were genuinely happy she'd been joined with her new mate, most were there simply to be privy to the events first hand.

Since her and Rylan's mating ceremony had been private, the celebration attendees would have to console themselves with seeing the couple engage in their first dance along with the traditional mate games held at such gatherings. Ophelia's most genuine smiles came along with the moments when her Glassmaker was earnestly trying to match her energy so they could be the winning couple in the somewhat silly tasks.

She didn't want to ruin it for Rylan by telling him they were guaranteed to win. It was tradition to let the newly mated triumph in the games. His serious commitment to each task was simply too endearing for her to intervene.

However, those bright spots were dampened by the looming uncertainty. She knew from the way her brothers rotated standing near them, that the strangers were likely among their guests. The whispered discussions between Rylan and Damien caused her to tense each time they put their heads together. It seemed once her brother understood the depth of Rylan's commitment to her, he became her mate's staunchest ally.

"Good rotation to you, Ophelia."

The saccharine sweet voice of Arwen Brightwater broke through Ophelia's musings. Looking at the other female, Ophelia pasted a cordial expression on her face. It was the most she could muster given the circumstances. No matter how pleasant her greeting, Arwen was anything but.

"Arwen, good rotation to you as well." Immediately getting to the point of the other female's presence, Ophelia clasped her hand around Rylan's large arm.

"Allow me to introduce my mate. This is Rylan of the Sunweavers. Rylan, meet Arwen of the Brightwaters."

Tilting his head down slightly, Rylan acknowledged the other female. "Pleasure."

As with Arwen, his word was polite, but it lacked the warmth of truth. Arwen extended her hand limply in a manner Ophelia was certain the other female considered queenly. Both she and Rylan simply stared at Arwen's outstretch limb. Once she realized Ophelia's mate wouldn't be falling to her feet in supplication, Arwen withdrew her fingers with an offended sniff.

However, Rylan's status as a Glassmaker put him above Arwen's station as a Phytokin mated to the son of a wealthy merchant. At least in Arwen's eyes. For as long as Ophelia had known her, Arwen had placed great importance on station and appearances. On the same rotation the Glassmaker declared Ophelia as unblessed, he'd read the sparks for Arwen.

As a Phytokin, Arwen was blessed with the ability to control plant life. Unlike Ramo's mate, Elara, who was capable of revitalizing a valley to produce lush vegetation, Arwen used her blessing as a low brow carnival performer might. She was content to have flowers blossom in any place her feet might touch. So, she constantly walked on a path of fragrant blooms.

Ophelia deduced it was no more than Arwen felt she deserved. If she couldn't actually be a queen, she could have petals strewn at her feet as if she were. Conversely, with the Leanders keeping mainly to themselves and not being completely accepted by the population in Misthaven, in Arwen's estimation, Ophelia was beneath her.

Arwen made no secret of her opinions of Ophelia being unblessed and unmated at more than thirty Winters old. It was good for Ophelia that she didn't give two rodents whiskers what Arwen of the Brightwaters thought of her. Ophelia had allowed her gaze to wander away from Arwen when the female spoke again, reminding Ophelia of her presence.

"How ever did you meet a Glassmaker, Phe—Ophelia?"

Ophelia's gazed narrowed causing the quick correction by Arwen. They weren't friends. She'd never tolerated such familiarity with shortening her name. Rather than answer Arwen's probing query, Ophelia asked one of her own.

"Where is your mate, Arwen? I would like to introduce my Rylan to him."

Arwen's cheeks pinkened beneath her honey bronzed skin. It was well known Arwen's mate spent many rotations 'traveling' to expand his father's merchant empire. She was often left to care for their offspring and household alone. At least she had nursemaids and staff to assist her. So, it wasn't a hardship. With the exception of it being clear her mate preferred the dust of the road to Arwen's presence that is.

Aware she was being spiteful, Ophelia couldn't even take a moment to enjoy Arwen's discomfort. A curious, nearly painful, feeling overcame her. It was as if something were attempting to peel at the edges of her mind with sharpened talons. Pushing against the sensation, Ophelia looked away from Arwen again. A twitch of her eye was the only indicator something was amiss, but it was apparently enough for Rylan to notice.

"Excuse us."

A brisk nod was his only gesture to Arwen before slipping an arm around Ophelia's waist, leading her away from the vapid female. As he swiftly led her out of the tent, Ophelia was aware of Jaime's presence trailing alongside them. When they were a safe distance from the crowd, Rylan stopped. His large hands shared his heat with her as he rested them on her shoulders.

"What is it, Sweeting?"

Furrowing her brow, Ophelia tried to find the words to explain what occurred. She gave no pretense to not knowing the source of his concern. When she attempted to explain it to him, she was uncertain if she'd expressed herself properly.

Placing her hands on her temples, she pushed against the sensation. While the feeling had dissipated, it remained. It no longer felt like scratching fingernails and was more of a probing sensation. After a few moments, it disappeared.

"Sweeting?"

Concern dripped from the endearment. Lifting her gaze to his, she managed a softer expression. Touching his hands where they remained on her shoulders, she tapped them lightly.

"It's gone now."

Rylan's look of concern persisted, despite her assurances. Ophelia smiled in an effort to soothe him further. His gaze lifted above her head prompting her to look behind her. Her father approached with Damien at his side.

Their demeanors projected concern. Around them, the sounds of revelers continued as though nothing untoward had occurred. But their small circle held a different air.

"Phely, tell Papa what happened."

Not questioning Jaime's directive, Ophelia turned to her father to recount what occurred. He listened without interruption until she was done. Only when she was finished did he speak.

"What were you doing when you first felt it?"

"I was talking to Arwen."

"Arwen?" Her father knew who Arwen was, his question was more of an indicator of his surprise.

"Yes. She approached us. I introduced her to Rylan. She asked how we met. It was when I asked her about her mate that I first experienced the feeling I told you about."

Her father's face gave nothing away as he nodded. "Do you recall seeing anyone near you? Anyone at all?"

Shaking her head, Ophelia looked to Rylan. "There was no one unfamiliar that I recall. Simply our neighbors from the village and younglings running about playing chase."

Rylan interjected when Ophelia paused to think further. "Most everyone here is a stranger to me, but I didn't notice anyone giving more attention than expected to Ophelia. Other than Arwen."

Frowning, Ophelia looked at her father. "Papa, what is it?"

"I believe there is a Glydder about. Possibly a Bender as well. The Bender is likely disguising them because none of us has detected a stranger as of yet."

This new information from her papa made the fine hair on Ophelia's arms stand on end. Glydders were known to slip into being's minds and cull information whether it be conscious or subconscious thoughts. That wasn't good. No visible strangers meant the misdirection regarding how she and Rylan came to be mated was all for naught. Almost immediately, her mother had begun spreading the story of Rylan courting Ophelia secretly.

She'd also intimated he'd faced the same issue as previous

Glassmakers, and had been unable to read the sparks for her. So, supposedly, he'd convinced her to stop trying some time ago. Ophelia was a very common name in the realm. So, even if Caspian had heard it, he wouldn't have an accurate physical description as Rylan and her brothers had taken great care to ensure he never saw her face.

It was thin, but they believed in it. Especially since only their close family knew of their recent journey to Thistledown. Neighbors were aware the siblings had traveled, but weren't privy as to where in the realm they'd gone. Her papa hoped their practice of keeping to themselves would aid them in the subterfuge.

Chapter Twenty-One

Rylan gave no care to pretense as he swept his gaze around the expanse of revelers milling in the field being used as the celebration site. He listened raptly to the elder Leander as he searched each face within his range of sight.

With none of the Leanders reporting having seen a stranger, and the elder stating his concern regarding a Bender, Rylan's vigilance had increased. The brothers began talking over one another as each tossed out possibilities given the new information. Unable to contribute, Rylan continued with his perusal of the crowd.

Despite Ophelia's assertion that her family kept to themselves, it appeared the entire village was present. Rylan spotted the female, Arwen, at the edge of the tent. Next to her was a youngling, from appearances no more than eight winters.

The two spoke animatedly. From their gestures, Rylan deduced they were discussing the toy in the young male's hand. His small face was bright with excitement as he held it up for her inspection. Another youngling ran to them, her long skirts trailing behind her in the breeze. The female who chased her looked mildly haggard when she came to a stop next to Arwen and the youngling.

Ophelia's light touch drew his attention back to her. Her face tilted up to his with a single eyebrow lifted in question.

"What is it, Rylan?"

"Nothing, Sweeting. I was simply observing."

"Observing what?"

Ophelia turned following the direction of his previous stare. A line appeared on her brow the longer she looked at Arwen. It was quite evident earlier there was no love lost between the two females. But, Ophelia seemed to be staring overly long.

"Sweeting?" Rylan placed his hand at Ophelia's back. A hush fell over the others as it became obvious something was amiss. When they began to crane their necks looking around, Ophelia tore her gaze away from Arwen.

"Don't! Don't stare."

"What is it, daughter?" Her father was the only one who hadn't been searching for the source of Ophelia's unease. Like Rylan, he'd been focused on Ophelia.

Turning away from the tent, Ophelia looked to her brother, Damien. "Please try not to be obvious, but observe Arwen. Does anything appear strange to you?"

Their group remained silent as they waited. After a few moments, Damien's facial expression shifted from the veil of concentration he'd worn to one of determination. At the shift, Ophelia began nodding.

"You see it too don't you? Or rather you don't see it."

"Yes." Damien confirmed.

"Are the rest of us allowed to know?" Jaime's question was delivered in a dry tone.

"The flowers." Damien said shortly.

"What about them? There are flowers everywhere. Elara made certain of it."

"Everywhere but beneath Arwen's feet." Damien lowered his voice further when he imparted that information.

Rylan wasn't certain why the detail was important, but from the darkness descending on each man's face, he was certain it was. Still, he broached the question.

"Should there be flowers at her feet?"

Ophelia nodded as she replied. "From the moment her blessing manifested, whenever Arwen's feet touch the earth, flowers bloomed."

Rylan didn't lift his head to confirm their assessment, he simply nodded. "Except now."

Ophelia's chin dipped. "Except for now."

Damien shifted to Rylan's left. "Which of them do you think is the Bender?" His stare was trained on his father as he awaited a response.

Shaking his head, their father looked in the opposite direction. "I'm not certain. But whoever it is, is more powerful than average."

Rylan searched the faces of the Leanders before returning his stare to Ophelia. "Am I to understand that the female who introduced herself earlier isn't Arwen of the Brightwaters?"

"Correct. And it's likely those aren't her offspring nor their caregiver. Arwen would never allow such public displays —even in a joyful setting. The young female is disheveled, while the young male has stains on his breeches from playing in the grass."

Ophelia relayed her observations without looking toward the tent. In fact, she smiled and waved at another couple who passed their group calling out greetings. To anyone observing them, they were simply chatting and taking a break from being in the crush of the merrymakers.

"I do believe we've found our strangers." Nodding to his sons, the elder Leander strode away.

The others, with the exception of Jaime followed suit.

Jaime remained close to Ophelia and Rylan. Though the start of the plan had gone awry, this part was proceeding according to script. Ramo, Kieran and Damien would relay the information to Ronan and Magnus who would assist in securing the strangers.

Since their disguise was now known, they'd have to be more cautious, but Rylan had no doubt the other males still intended to escort the strangers to the designated location. Keeping up the appearance of the happy couple, Rylan and Ophelia rejoined the festivities. His Sweeting didn't complain further about probing pains, but Rylan remained on alert for the imposters.

Musicians played a jaunty tune as Rylan danced Ophelia away from the cluster of bodies swaying and twirling to the melody. She offered no resistance, following his lead until they were able to stop dancing and walk at a moderate pace into the tall trees bordering the celebration field. Jaime had finally given them the signal regarding their uninvited guests. So, Rylan and Ophelia were going to the designated meeting place.

This was the part of the plan Rylan didn't like at all, but his Sweeting wouldn't be swayed. She wanted to be present citing the possibility of her being able to assist with the use of her gift. Having witnessed the power of her blessing, untrained, Rylan didn't doubt her ability. However, she lacked control due to inexperience. It could very well spell disaster.

But, he was quickly learning there was very little he could deny his Sweeting. Therefore, they traipsed through the foliage until they reached the small clearing. Several of the Leanders, their kin and a few trusted friends were posted around the space. At the center were the beings still posing as Arwen, her offspring and their caregiver.

Unlike previously, the imposter Arwen's perfectly coiffed hair now stuck out at odd angles from the once neatly arranged hairstyle. There was a tear in the shoulder of the gown and one of her velvet slippers was missing. The younglings were in a similar state as was the caregiver. Although Rylan should stop thinking of them as younglings, since it was likely they were full adults in disguise.

"Why are you doing this?"

Imposter Arwen's tear-filled voice cracked to accompany the wetness gathering in her dark eyes. The young male and female huddled against the caregiver's sides as if it had finally occurred to them that they should display more affection toward this female than the one pretending to be their mother.

"Cease with the theatrics!"

Theron's words boomed, nearly shaking the otherwise quiet space. The Changer's lion seemed precariously close to the surface with the growled command.

"We know you aren't Arwen, just as we know those are not your younglings and *she* is not the caregiver for the Brightwater younglings." Slowly advancing on the four of them, he continued. "The question remains, who are you? And, who sent you?"

"Theron Leander, you know me. I have lived in this village for my entire life. Why are you accusing me of being someone else? I don't understand."

Whoever the Bender was, they were quite skilled. The inflections in the female's voice would've normally caused many males to relent—apologizing profusely. However, keeping up this level of illusion had to be wearing on them. His suspicion was confirmed when Ophelia's fingers gripped his. Tugging on his arm, she rose to her tip-toes to whisper in his ear.

"Did you see that?"

Replying just as softly, he looked from her face to the beings at the center of their circle. "See what, Sweeting?"

"It was a flash of something...else. Someone...else...Then, Arwen and the others were there again."

"I did not."

Rylan glanced toward the huddled beings again before returning his attention to his mate. An idea had formed. He allowed his instinct to lead him.

"Did you feel anything when you saw the flash of...others?"

"Anything like what?" Ophelia's brow creased in concentration.

Clasping her hands in his, Rylan captured her full attention. Blocking out the sound of Theron continuing to question the imposters, Rylan held only Ophelia in his sight.

"Do you recall when you assisted Ramo? You said you could feel the energy of his blessing like waves bouncing around you. Earlier, when the Glydder attempted to access your thoughts, you experienced a clawing sensation."

Ophelia's face brightened as Rylan's idea took hold. When she nodded, he knew no further prodding was necessary. Shaking her hands to release them from his she rotated toward the cowering group. Her continence went through several shifts, but she remained silent.

He didn't have to wonder if she was able to locate the energy trail. It was as if her aura radiated more brightly than it had the first time he saw her. Rylan didn't understand how the others were able to stand around them as if it wasn't becoming blindingly bright in the small clearing.

A hideous screech snapped his attention from his magnificent mate. Visually searching the area, he located the source of the sound. At the center of their circle, where imposter Arwen and the others previously stood, were four adult males. A collective gasp swept through the group.

"What in the cursed river?..." One of the Leander males asked. Rylan didn't look to see which one, as his focus had returned to his mate.

The blinding brightness of her aura had dimmed and she swayed slightly. Slipping an arm around her, he tugged her close allowing her to lean on him and draw from his strength.

"How did they—"

Ophelia's father cut across the person speaking. "It matters not how, or what. We now have our answer as to who these imposters really are."

It took a moment for all but one of the pretenders to realize the veil of illusion had been stripped away. The one who wasn't surprised, collapsed into a heap at the feet of the males who'd, sands before, worn the faces of the Brightwater younglings.

Chapter Twenty-Two

"Jaime." The commanding voice of Ophelia's father penetrated the slight fog which had descended on her.

After finding the Bender's energy trail and somehow breaking through the illusion he'd created, her own energy stores were temporarily diminished. Although, she could feel her strength returning. It was occurring much more swiftly than it had when she'd assisted Ramo. She could only conclude it took more effort to hide their large entourage than it did to break the veil the Bender had placed over their vision.

Through half-lidded eyes, she watched as her brother quickly stepped forward. While the presumed Bender remained on the forest floor, Jaime grasped the others. Only his grip on one of the males slipped as he shifted into a large bird. Jaime's responding roar reminded Ophelia of her father's lion.

Screeching cries rang out into the otherwise quiet clearing as the Changer's wings flapped taking them farther away— leaving the scraps of their garments at Jaime's feet. While her brothers expressed their anger that one of the strangers had fled, Ophelia was concerned with the implications of said escape. Rylan's normally erect posture was even more stiff, indicating he shared her sentiments. They'd quickly become connected. And while they couldn't read one another's thoughts, words weren't necessary for her to discern his demeanor.

"Damien, Ramo, secure the others. Make certain to cover their eyes. Do the same to the Glydder. We don't want him in our heads until we're ready."

It had been barely a few minor sands since the Changer had flown off, but her papa recovered quickly enough to contain the situation. While Kieran, Ronan, and Magnus walked the periphery to make certain their gathering was still private, her papa began interrogating their unwanted guests.

The weight of Rylan's arm around her waist not only gave Ophelia comfort, but also seemed to help her regain her strength sooner. Even after she felt more like herself, she leaned into his side while she watched her father ply information from the conscious members of Caspian's small group of spies.

The longer it took to get information, the more concerned she grew about the Changer who escaped. She didn't doubt he was returning to his employer. While she was no expert on falcons, she did know they could cover great distances very quickly. It made them ideal scouts, but put her and her family at a disadvantage. Their journey of several rotations between Misthaven and Thistledown could be completed in far less time by the large bird of prey.

"If you desire to see another rotation in this realm, you will talk and you will do it now."

Ophelia watched her father as he leaned closer to male he'd determined was the Glydder, who was now bound hand and foot. All three were similarly trussed with their backs pressed together in a triangle formation. The Bender was now conscious, but wasn't speaking. Neither was the third male of unknown blessing. Contrary to how it appeared, the Glydder spoke. He simply wasn't saying the things any of them wanted to hear.

"I have told you, Leander. I do not know any Caspian. My friends and I are simply travelers."

"Simple travelers do not take on the appearance of a well-known merchant's wife and younglings."

"They do if they do not want to attract attention which is normally visited on strangers." In Ophelia's opinion, the Glydder's voice held too much confidence for one in such a precarious position.

Damien's response to his cheeky retort was immediate. "The only strangers who would concern themselves with being noticed are ones with wicked intentions."

Damien stood next to her father giving the males his full attention. Her Seeker brother could find anything, but Ophelia wasn't sure if his blessing extended to ferreting out information. Over the last rotations she'd come to terms with the wealth of things still beyond her comprehension in regards to blessings from the goddess.

"Enough of this!" Frustration was evident in Jaime's declaration. Stepping into the Glydder's space, he used one hand to lift the male from the ground by the front of his garments. Seeing as they were all tied together, the other two dangled from the Glydder's bound body.

Ripping the blindfold from the Glydder's eyes, Jaime shook them adding emphasis to his words. The mind-reader's eyes widened. Jaime's strength was evident in him performing the task without so much as a grunt or a bead of sweat on his teak brown brow.

"Look at me, Glydder. Read my thoughts and know what I'm saying is true. If you do not tell us what we want to know, you will breathe your last breath on this packed dirt."

Without reading his mind, Ophelia didn't doubt Jaime's

threat. The Brawn was slow to anger, but his fierce loyalty to his family meant no one who threatened them was safe from his wrath. For him to willingly allow a Glydder to probe his mind also said he would truly honor his words to the other male.

The bobbing lump in the stranger's neck was proceeded by him slamming his eyes shut. Apparently, Jaime's thoughts were more than he cared to deal with.

"I yield! I yield, but I truly don't know his plan! We were simply sent out to find the Ergokin. We had no information other than the colors she wore and themaleswho accompanied her. I pledge to you, that is all I know. That's all."

Replacing the blind fold, her papa gestured for Jaime to lower them back to a seated position.

"Who sent you?" Although they knew the answer, her father asked anyway.

"Caspian. Caspian of the Ironshades."

Even with their advance knowledge of his search for her, Ophelia stiffened upon hearing his name. Beside her, Rylan's form became harder than steel. Having not contributed to the interrogation, his voice caused every head to turn in his direction.

"How many? How many of you were sent to hunt an innocent being?"

The threat of punishment was conveyed in his tone. Ophelia was sure it only added to the terror induced by the Glydder's peek into Jaime's thoughts. The male responded without hesitation.

"I don't know! I say this in truth. Caspian has many to do his bidding. He only tells us what he deems necessary to perform our tasks."

"And what were you to do if you located the Ergokin?"

The Bender jerked to awareness, hissing at his comrade before he could respond to Rylan's question. "Shut your mouth you weakling! You know what he does to those who betray him."

"Jaime."

Ophelia's gaze snapped to her father who calmly instructed her brother with only the mention of his name. Her sense of trepidation increased at the Bender's sudden outburst. She had no illusion of Caspian as a kind or benevolent being, but the abject fear shaking the Bender's frame spoke well beyond the words he uttered.

Following their father's unspoken directive, Jaime shoved a cloth into the Bender's mouth, sealing it with a longer length of similar material. Once he was done, he thumped the male's forehead with his fist. The action rendered the male unconscious once again. Instead of standing to his full height, Jaime leaned over to the other two males.

"This one is afraid of a master you cannot see, when he should be worried about the males surrounding you right now." Leaning over to look only at the Glydder, he continued. "Maybe it's because he didn't see what you saw when you probed my thoughts. You remember don't you? The things I pledge to do to you and your friends?"

The weather was mild, so Ophelia was certain the Glydder's shivers couldn't be from the cold. She determined it was best she not wonder too deeply about her brother's dark thoughts. It was best left unseen if it caused the road hardened male to visibly quake with fear.

When the Glydder didn't respond, Jaime nudged him in the chest. "You do remember don't you?"

"Ye—" The male's voice cracked mid-word. Clearing his throat, he tried again. "Yes. I remember."

"So, talk." Rylan barked the command with such force, Ophelia jumped slightly.

While he immediately moved to soothe her, she noticed his gaze never left the bound trio. When the Glydder spoke again, he didn't have to be prodded to give additional information. He told them everything he knew about Caspian—from how vast his lands were outside of Thistledown, to the number of women he called his life mates housed there, as well as what happened to anyone who attempted to leave to start their own lives.

Listening to him, Ophelia felt a twinge of pity toward the Glydder. Being under Caspian's control was the only life he'd ever known. The restrictiveness and total control were very likely in the plan the older male had for her. Ophelia's heart thudded in her ears as everything she'd heard and all that had come to pass seem to close in on her.

Considering his wealth, vast holdings and minions at his command, her concerns were valid. As if he sensed the path of her thoughts, Rylan gathered her in his embrace. Pressing a kiss to her forehead, he murmured in her ear.

"Do not fret, Sweeting. Caspian will never touch a strand of your beautiful hair, nor any other part of you."

Chapter Twenty-Three

Rylan meant every word spoken to his Sweeting. Even as his blood boiled hotter than a Glassmaker's furnace, he made certain she understood he would protect her with his life. She was his mate. The few rotations they'd known one another didn't matter. She was his, just as he was hers.

The way he isolated himself from the goings on in Thistledown had insulated him from the depths of Caspian's dealings. His original dislike of the male stemmed mainly from his gut instincts. It had grown to a more than healthy distrust which was why he wanted Ophelia away from him as quickly as possible. Even though Rylan had known the male was dangerous, his knowledge had only been a modicum of what was truly there.

"We must leave. Now."

Rylan wasn't making a suggestion and no one contradicted what he said. The Leander and his sons wore identical expressions to Rylan's. The Changer who'd flown off could very well be passing along confirmation of Ophelia's whereabouts and her blessing to Caspian.

The spies had been in Misthaven long enough to know the

Leanders were still considered by some to be outsiders. Rylan had no doubt Caspian would attempt to use the information to his advantage. Plans to protect their holdings and get his Sweeting to the one being who might possibly be able to help her master her blessing, would need to be accelerated.

Praises to the goddess that he met with no resistance from his mate. The spies were spirited away to be dealt with by trusted Leander family members while the already prepared horses were brought to the far side of the keep. The revelers remained in the field, blissfully unaware of the machinations going on right under their noses.

Rylan stood ramrod straight next to his Sweeting as she bid her parents goodbye. Her papa was stoic, his gaze penetrating Rylan with a very clear message. Her mama's eyes held a sheen of tears as she pulled Ophelia to her countless times while dispensing advice and whispering loving words.

"Mama, we have to go." Ophelia finally put an end to the hugging. "You and papa have to go back to the party to keep the festivities going. Remember that everyone must believe we simply snuck away to the mating cabin to begin our period of togetherness."

"I know. I know." The tears she'd held at bay finally spilled down her mother's cheeks. Swiping at them, she nodded firmly before stepping back from Ophelia.

Taking the opening, Rylan guided his Sweeting to her mount and assisted her in taking her seat in the saddle. With one final glance at the Leander, Rylan adjusted the weapons strapped to his back and mounted his own steed. Shadowfox danced lightly under his weight, but quickly settled.

"We will return." Rylan issued his declaration with confidence. Nodding to those assembled, he urged his mount in the direction they'd agreed led to the safest route to the Keeper.

Their group was small, which would allow them to move quickly. Damien was the only one of Ophelia's brothers to accompany them, along with their cousin through mating, Magnus. The others would be needed for any possible disturbance in Misthaven.

However, having Damien and Magnus would be more than enough. While he wasn't a Qarikin like Ramo, as an Earther, Magnus was able to obscure their physical impressions on the earth. They'd have to be mindful of other ways they'd leave a trail, but it would still take a skilled Seeker to follow them.

Damien led their small entourage while Magnus brought up the rear. They'd been riding at a decent pace for a while when Ophelia spoke. Rylan knew the events of the rotation were weighing on her. But he also was innately aware that she wouldn't speak on anything until she was ready.

"We can't wait until I reach the Keeper for me to begin working on using my blessing. There is no guarantee she'll be able to help me, and I need to be able to defend myself better without requiring a nap afterwards."

Nodding, Rylan agreed with her. "What would you like to do, Sweeting? We only have Damien and Magnus with us, but I do not see them refusing to assist you."

"You can help too, Glassmaker."

Rylan stared into Ophelia's golden gaze. Her assertion had been the farthest thing from his mind.

"Sweeting, I will always help you in whatever way possible. I am simply not sure how I can in this instance. I read the sparks. Without a furnace, glass and a potential being present, how could I do any of those things?"

"Glassmaker, isn't your ability to read the sparks a gift from the goddess? Did you not have to stand before a Glassmaker to receive the knowledge of your blessing—your path?"

Rylan clamped his lips closed as he considered her words. She wasn't wrong. However, since reading the sparks appeared to be the most active part of his blessing, he didn't consider it the same as the others he'd proclaimed over the revolutions.

In the quiet moments which passed after her thought-provoking questions, he recalled what occurred when they first met. How he'd essentially seen the same colors surrounding her that had shot from the cooling glass when he'd read the sparks a few scant sands later. Had she been using her blessing even then—amplifying his own?

"If you believe I can be of help in the absence of a furnace and tools, I will not turn you away, Sweeting."

"Good." Her demeanor shifted to almost cheerful. Turning her attention to the trail before them, she went silent for a few beats.

Rylan followed suit. Instead of focusing only on the path, he attuned his senses to their surroundings. The *trail* they traveled wasn't a true beaten path, but one Damien picked for them using his Seeker instincts. The only noises reaching his ears were the sounds from their mounts. The occasional huff or neigh. Ophelia finally spoke again breaking through the silence.

"In my family, there are many different blessings. But I don't know of an Ergokin in the Leander line nor the Night-shades, my mama's family line. They don't talk about how their blessings work. They simply use them as one would breathe or speak."

Turning slightly toward him in her saddle, she pierced him with an expression of curiosity. "Does it work the same for you? Is the process the same as breathing?"

"In some ways." Rylan chose his next words carefully. "Working the glass is a learned skill, which is why Glassmakers must apprentice before being allowed to seek out their own village to serve. We can all read the sparks, but not all Glass-makers create vessels or other pieces beyond the reading."

"They don't?"

143

Rylan understood Ophelia's confusion. One room of their massive home held cabinetry which had several pieces of blown glass on display. Some simple, while others were intricate. Each, he'd learned, were the pieces presented to the blessed family members following the reading of their sparks. In his Sweeting's world, having the physical representation of one's blessing was a part of the package.

"No, Sweeting. Your family has been fortunate to have access to a very skilled Glassmaker." Reading the twist of her lips, he chuckled. "We cannot count his inability to read the sparks for you. You are a unique being. Many others failed after him."

Rylan wasn't simply defending the unknown Glassmaker; he was speaking the truth as he knew it. The works on display at the Leander keep were quality pieces rendered by a skilled artisan.

The two dropped into silence once again as Rylan considered her question. When searching his memory for an answer didn't produce the desired results, he had another idea. Damien rode approximately five lengths ahead of them. Rylan regarded his mate's brother as if the male had just entered his workshop requesting a reading.

When he did so, he had to clasp his mount's reins tighter in his hands and grip his thighs to keep from falling from the massive beast. Shades of orange radiated from Damien's form. Since they were traveling in a heavily shaded route, it couldn't be blamed on a trick of the sun. Besides, Rylan knew orange was the primary color in the sparks for Seekers.

Tempering his surprise at tapping into his blessing in the absence of his tools, he did what he'd instructed his mate to do earlier in the clearing. He followed the thread until he landed on the source. It was the opening of his senses and study of another being.

So, Ophelia's first lesson began with Rylan instructing her

on the way Glassmakers did those very things using their instincts to guide their hands in the selection of the elements needed to produce the physical manifestation of a being's blessing. A quick study, his Sweeting followed his lead to the point that when he turned his gaze on Magnus, he immediately saw the shades of brown emanating from the other male's burly form. She'd not only discovered the thread, she'd magnified his gift several times over.

"Good goddess, Sweeting." Rylan heard the whispered awe in his voice. Ophelia's bright smile was her only response.

Chapter Twenty-Four

Instead of feeling drained as she'd felt during previous targeted uses of her blessing, Ophelia felt exhilarated. She wasn't certain if she could attribute it to Rylan's gentle guidance, or their connection. But, it was as if she could see the deep blue color radiating from him as he explained how he'd tapped into his blessing to allow her to find the source. The energy was charged. Almost crackling as if flames were consuming dry kindling.

Damien's voice drew her out of the pleasant bubble her accomplishment created around them.

"We should stop here for the night. There's fresh water nearby and the trees offer good coverage to keep us from being discovered."

There were no complaints to her brother's suggestion. Instead, everyone dismounted. Magnus knelt until his fingertips were lost in the grass touching the ground beneath them. Ophelia didn't know his intentions. But wanting to be useful, she quickly honed in on the telltale signs of his blessing being used. Instinctively, she stretched one hand in his direction.

The foliage surrounding them became denser and the trees

seemed to move closer together creating a nearly impenetrable wall. The only opening in the barrier led in the direction of the water source Damien mentioned. When he stood to his feet, Magnus turned toward her wearing an indiscernible expression. He never spoke, but as he cared for his horse, he occasionally sent curious glances in her direction.

Happy she hadn't felt more than a slight twinge of fatigue, Ophelia simply grinned. Gathering her water pouch, she tried to collect pouches from the others, volunteering to fill them. Damien quickly disallowed the idea taking the leather vessels from her.

"Magnus and I will water the horses and fill these. You and your mate prepare for our evening meal." Looking toward Rylan he lifted one eyebrow. "You can start a fire outside of your furnace, correct."

"No. I've never created fire a rotation in my life." Rylan's dry and obviously false response caused a chuckle from Ophelia's older brother.

"We'll return shortly."

Rylan's response was a grunt while Ophelia giggled at their antics. It pleased her to know her mate and her brother had forged a relationship of their own. It gave her hope for the future of their union.

With the looming threat and their quest to get to the Keeper, she and Rylan hadn't discussed what their mating would mean in regards to where they would reside. While it was common for females to return with their mates to their village, it was not unheard of for the males to join the females.

She allowed the thought only a moment before she set about gathering wood pieces dry enough to start a fire. Rylan was placing stones and turning over earth while she searched. They wouldn't require a lot of wood as they couldn't afford to have a large fire. Simply enough to keep them warm during the coldest portion of the night.

By the time they were done, Magnus and Damien had returned. She noted Magnus's wheat-colored tresses were wet. They'd traveled at a moderate pace, and off road. But Ophelia still felt as if road dust had insinuated beneath her garments. So, when she accepted Starlight's reins from Magnus, she asked him about the water source.

"Is the water suitable for bathing? Is it warm?"

"It's no match for the pulls in the keep, but it isn't frigid." His eyes lit up when he imparted his next bit of information. "There's a waterfall."

The youthful note of wonder in his voice drew a smile from Ophelia. A waterfall sounded amazing. Tending to her horse, she attached the feed bag as quickly as she could. She couldn't wait to stand beneath the cascading falls. No matter what Damien said, Ophelia was determined to experience its magic.

Gathering what she needed from her bag, she stood with her arms loaded and a look of defiance on her face.

"I'm going to clean up." Looking at her brother, she silently dared him to object. Instead, he looked from her to Rylan.

"Am I to assume you'll accompany your mate?" Dropping to his haunches, Damien began extracting food from one of their meal packs.

Warmth from Rylan's body heated Ophelia's right side as he stopped next to her, removing the weight of the parcels from her arms.

"Of course I will attend my Sweeting." Rylan's response was accompanied by the weight of his hand on her back.

While Ophelia was shocked by her brother's immediate acquiescence, she wasn't one to question good fortune. Quickly making their exit, she and Rylan passed through the opening in their tree barrier, following the sounds of the rushing water.

A cool breeze lifted the hair at her nape as soon as they left the cover of their constructed sanctuary. The melodic symphony created by the water splashing against the stones was much louder. Ophelia's gaze was drawn to the sky just above the top of the falls. It was painted in shades of purple, orange and yellow. The first twinkling of stars peeked through the gentle haze.

"This is beautiful."

"Not nearly as beautiful as you, my mate."

Ophelia tore her gaze away from the vibrant sky to peer up at Rylan. She hadn't missed the gruff timbre of his voice. She remembered it well from their moments of coitus over the past two rotations. The sound immediately sent tingles to her nether regions. Squeezing her knees together offered little relief from the growing ache.

When Rylan's lips stretched into a knowing grin, Ophelia knew her attempts to tamp down her desire were futile. Taking her hand, her mate silently led her to a path she hadn't noticed in her perusal of the cascading water. Trust was in each footfall she made onto the narrow trail leading behind the waterfall.

They came to a stop in a small alcove with the tumbling water serving as a curtain between them and the rest of the small lagoon. Her gaze was glued to her mate as he placed her things on a large stone just inside the entry to the nook. After his hands moved to unfasten the straps holding his weapons to his back, her heartbeat picked up—pounding in her ears and at her core.

Her initial fascination with the specially crafted sword and axe was diminished by the flexing of his muscles as he performed the relatively mundane task. When he'd reached the point of removing his shirt, she remained just as he'd left her, transfixed.

"Do you require assistance, Sweeting?"

The rough quality of his voice scraped over her senses, but Ophelia need not have worried about supplying an answer. Rylan was at her side in an instant, releasing the laces holding the bodice of her blouse closed. Her clothing wasn't an adequate barrier to keep his questing fingers at bay.

Although, halting his progress was the furthest thing from her mind. As they had been trained during her short time mated to the Glassmaker, her digits gravitated to his large form, assisting with relieving him of his garments as he performed the same task for her.

Once she stood before him bare, there were scant sands before she was folded into his arms. The hair on his chest and torso tickled her nipples and her cheek as she nuzzled between his pectorals before lifting her face to his in anticipation of his kiss. Rylan didn't disappoint her. He immediately captured her lips. Separating long enough to grunt a command for her to hold on, he reclaimed her mouth as he lifted her from her feet.

Recalling the position, she wrapped her legs around him just as he impaled her with his thickness. Ophelia's eyelids slid closed with the feeling of bliss coursing through her. She had no idea if mating relations were the same for other females, but she felt feral in her desire to have him claim her over and over.

Her already slick channel was flooded with more of her natural lubricant as Rylan shuttled his length in and out of her quivering walls. He captured her keening moans with his continued kiss. Coolness from the stone wall met her back, lightly abrading her skin as Rylan balanced her there. The moment was the precursor to him tunneling into her flower with precision which soon flung her into the abyss of her release.

His mouth was the receptacle for her cries of completion as he maintained their connection through her cresting into his own. Ophelia twitched from the after effects of her orgasm as well as the feeling of his turgid length jerking within her channel. He pushed his own groans of fulfillment into her mouth while he shot his seed into her grasping depths.

They remained joined for a short while, not disconnecting until their breathing returned to normal. Once he was certain she was steady on her feet, Rylan helped Ophelia to a separate cascading section of the waterfall where they both washed themselves quickly. Contrary to Magnus's assertion, the water was indeed frigid. But she was able to adjust to it hastily in order to complete the bathing process.

By the time she and Rylan returned to the others, Damien was wrapped in a blanket lying on his bedroll. After they were securely inside, Magnus closed the opening in the trees before lying on his own sleeping mat.

Ophelia fell asleep that night as she had each night since mating with Rylan, in his embrace. The hard ground beneath them didn't detract from her comfort and she soon slipped into repose.

Chapter Twenty-Five

When they'd set out to seek an audience with the Keeper of the Blessings, Rylan had been sure it was what was best for Ophelia and the nurturing of her blessing. The longer the journey took, and the aura of impending conflict hovering above them made him reconsider.

Should he have simply treated it like any other spark reading and given the information to the Chronicler in Thistledown? Or should they have used the one in Misthaven, as it was the land of his Sweeting's birth? He was no longer certain if doing so would have made her any more or less of a target than she was currently.

Damien selected a route which kept them from interacting with others with any frequency, but there were times when it was unavoidable. Despite Rylan's growing concerns, their journey wasn't melancholy or constantly tension fraught. That was due in large part to Ophelia and her joy in her growth in the understanding of her blessing.

Each night as they made camp and for a little while after, she worked with Magnus and Damien. She listened attentively when they described the feeling of having their natural abilities augmented. It was during one of the sessions when they discovered, if she physically made contact with a being actively using their gift, she experienced something of a transfer.

It didn't last long, but for a few moments after, she was able to use their blessing as if it were her own. This resulted in the formation of a crater between her feet when she'd touched Magnus in the process of him hiding their campsite by shifting stone and earth.

"Goddess keep me!"

Ophelia jumped back from the hole which appeared at her feet. Rylan was at her side immediately, folding her into his arms. Her heart beat so hard and rapidly, even he felt the pounding thumps.

"What is it, Sweeting?"

Pointing mutely at the large crater he'd pulled her away from, Ophelia's mouth worked without producing words.

"Phely?" Damien approached them slowly, his face a mask of concern. Magnus stood at his side with a similar expression.

After a few moments of Rylan holding and soothing her, She was finally able to give voice to her thoughts.

"I did that. I don't know how, but I did it."

Looking from her to the deep impression in the earth, Magnus knelt pressing his hand to the ground.

"It's okay, Phely. I can fix it. Look."

Before their eyes, the concave appearance of the soil evened out until it was as if nothing had ever occurred. Ophelia's breathing returned to normal and her eyes took on a glint Rylan was beginning to know well. She now wanted answers.

The remainder of the evening was spent testing this new aspect of her blessing. Rylan finally put a stop to it, citing their need to rest for the early rise planned to remain ahead of any potential pursuers.

The swiftness with which Ophelia became accustomed to recognizing the blessed when they encountered others nearly had Rylan convinced she'd been unconsciously utilizing her blessing for the majority of her life. He didn't mention it to her, but he held out hope that their visit to the Keeper wouldn't be fruitless.

Rylan was dragged from his thoughts by Damien's sudden stop. The skin on Rylan's forearm pebbled as he searched for the source of the other male's unease. The shrieking cry of a bird of prey pierced the silence and Rylan immediately understood the abrupt halt.

"Is it him?" Concern dripped from Ophelia's voice as she too turned her gaze to the sky.

"I don't know, Sweeting." Rylan's reply was delivered with regret.

Damien tried, as often as he could, to have them travel in forests and tree covered spaces. It wasn't always possible. This was one such time. They had no way of knowing what had come to pass since they'd left Misthaven. No way to ascertain if their guests had been convinced by the tale the Leanders wove about Rylan and Ophelia slipping away to enjoy their period of togetherness.

His instincts said no rumors meandering through the village would deter Caspian after hearing from his spy. Rylan's sudden departure from his workshop would've definitely been noticed. At a minimum, the Chronicler in Thistledown would sound an alarm when he didn't hear from Rylan to update the records of the blessings he declared. Since they spoke regularly, the Chronicler would be suspicious of his absence. He'd left in such haste he didn't leave so much as a missive to explain his absence.

"We need cover." Damien's suggestion was easily made, but not so easily remedied.

Magnus was an Earther. The only reason he was able to give them tree cover each night was because there were trees already in existence that could be manipulated using the soil.

He wasn't a Phytokin. He couldn't make anything grow where it didn't already exist. He required at least a seed.

The only cover he could possibly create would be by shifting the earth itself, which would only draw more attention to them, enclosing them, impeding their progress. No. They'd need to find another way to get out of the open. Without Ramo, or another Qarikin, they couldn't hide in plain sight.

Nudging their mounts to move faster, they all leaned low on their horses as they sped through the meadow. Rylan felt, more than saw, the atmosphere around them shift. When Damien's steed reared up on its hind legs, nearly unseating him, Rylan was forced to veer off to one side to keep from colliding with him as he gripped the reins in an attempt to stop Shadowfox without experiencing the same fate.

His immediate thought was of his Sweeting. Whipping around, his eyes wildly scanned their surroundings looking for her. He was able to swallow the lump in his throat when he saw she'd fared much better in bringing Starlight to a halt. As he brought his mount around, he located the reason for Damien's sudden stop.

Less than thirty lengths in front of them was what appeared to be a well-equipped band of mercenaries. Some carried swords sheathed at their waists, while others used harnesses similar to the one Rylan wore. They easily outnumbered Rylan and the others three to one.

At the center of the assembled barrier of beings was Caspian. The bright smile on his face was in direct contrast with the sinister air surrounding his appearance. Rylan only had to consider for a moment how he and the others seemed to appear out of nowhere. There must be a Traveler among them.

However, Rylan had only ever met Travelers who could transport themselves from one place to another with a thought. He'd never encountered one who possessed the ability to carry one passenger, let alone almost a dozen others. Just like his Sweeting, Rylan had become more adept at seeing the kaleidoscope of colors surrounding the blessed. So, he easily determined there was not one, but two Travelers in Caspian's cohort.

Guiding his mount closer to Ophelia's, Rylan reached behind him, placing one hand on the grip of the axe he'd forged himself. It wasn't simply a stunning testament to his craftsmanship as a Glassmaker, but a formidable weapon.

In one smooth motion, he removed it from his harness and flipped it so that the handle landed in his open palm. He didn't spare Damien nor Magnus a glance when they drew their own weapons. He'd ceased to be surprised by his mate who unsheathed her own short sword and dagger.

"Glassmaker! What a surprise! I do not recall us being enemies. Yet, you and your friends have drawn your weapons."

Caspian spread his arms out in what would normally be a welcoming gesture. To Rylan's eyes, it was a motion to display his might in numbers and blessings. He wasn't fooled by Caspian's fake gregariousness. He didn't have Travelers bring him there simply to be friendly.

Since Caspian addressed him and not the others, it was up to Rylan to respond.

"We were not enemies. And it doesn't have to be so, if you and your...friends would simply allow us to pass. We will continue to our destination while you do the same."

"My friend—"

"I said we were not enemies. I never said I was your friend." Rylan's voiced carried the sharp edge of steel as he intended.

A fleeting look of disgust flashed across Caspian's visage before he wiped it away. Clearing his throat, with a new even more phony smile plastered on his face, he made another attempt.

"This doesn't have to be contentious, Glassmaker. We both know why I am here. Simply give me the Ergokin and we can end this without conflict."

Looking around at his assembled group, he dropped his congenial façade when he turned back to Rylan and the others.

"I *will* take her by force, if necessary. You don't really want that do you? My friends and I would prefer not to injure any of you." He paused, tilting his head to one side. "But...we will, if you refuse to cooperate."

"You can drown in the river of the damned or be consumed by a dragon's flame for all I care. I will deliver you there myself before I allow you to touch my mate. So, the answer is no. I will not simply hand her over to you."

"Your mate?"

Caspian's attempt to sound surprised didn't fool Rylan. There was no way his spy hadn't passed along the information about their mating. So certain of his estimation, Rylan didn't bother to elaborate. He didn't foresee it having much impact. It was a waste of energy which would only play into whatever plan Caspian had constructed.

Chapter Twenty-Six

Movement to Rylan's right, drew Ophelia's attention. Damian was maneuvering his horse to stand alongside him while Magnus did the same on her left. Being one of very few females in a family of males didn't mean Ophelia had been coddled. On the contrary, her father had made certain she was more than capable with a blade and bow. While she wasn't eager to engage in battle, she wouldn't willingly go with Caspian—or anyone else.

That the male thought it was perfectly acceptable to demand she be handed over made her blood boil. She wished harder than ever she'd been aware of her abilities sooner. If she had, Ophelia could've become more proficient in the use of her blessing rather than still learning all of her capabilities.

Mentally shaking away the thought, Ophelia focused on the situation at hand. She couldn't dwell on what didn't come to pass. Besides, had the first Glassmaker read her sparks, she may never have met Rylan. Her Glassmaker had captured her heart and mind in a way none other had before him. Ophelia realized she wouldn't trade coming to her blessing sooner for meeting and mating with him.

As Rylan and the others positioned themselves to defend her, Ophelia's mind raced as she tried to figure out how she could help. She wasn't certain even the strength of her blessing would be to their advantage. Not when she'd only recently gained purpose with her control and only in the arena of amplifying or borrowing the abilities of another.

While Caspian spoke to Rylan, Ophelia scanned the males standing to either side of him. Caspian himself radiated a grayish hue indicating his status as a Ferrokin. There wasn't one among the baker's dozen assembled who did not carry the aura of the blessed. From Travelers to Seekers to Brawns and Changers, Caspian had assembled a menagerie, designed to assist him in achieving his goal—procuring her as if she weren't a living being. Like she was a thing. The very idea was repugnant. So much so, she felt compelled to voice it.

"It matters not why you are here. No one has the authority to *give* me over to *anyone*. I am not a *thing* to be bartered. I am a living being who breathes, thinks, and knows her own mind."

If anyone in her group was surprised she spoke up, they didn't allow it to be seen. Anger pulsed off Ophelia in waves. A sensation between a tingle and a buzzing skated across her skin. She watched as Caspian's mask slipped completely and fury blanketed his features. It was in stark contrast to the silky tone of his voice when he next spoke.

"Perhaps you want to reconsider your stance. My males will tell you. I'm quite generous to all my life mates. You. You're special, Ergokin. You would move right into the number one position. You will simply require a little...training."

The hazy gray color emanating from his slight frame grew clearer. The short sword in her right hand grew heavy to the point she was forced to drop it. A moment later, the same thing happened with the dagger in her left. She had no doubt

Caspian was the cause. The menacing grin he wore was confirmation.

Sensing the danger and tension of the moment, their horses began to dance nervously causing each of them to use a portion of their focus to calm the animals. Leaving the saddle wasn't an option. Engaging larger numbers on foot wasn't a good battle strategy. Regardless of the number of revolutions since the Leanders participated in actual battle, everyone was trained in combat and strategy.

Somewhere in the recesses of her memory, Ophelia recalled the countless discussions she'd had surrounding being an Ergokin. Since Rylan read her sparks, it had often been the topic of conversation. Ophelia had been assured that as she grew in her abilities, the possibilities of what she could do with them were limitless.

Please goddess. Show me what to do. Ophelia mouthed the small prayer as she stared into the face of evil. She had no doubt her mate and her family would sacrifice themselves to protect her. But, the thought of such actions was untenable to her. Despite her uncertainty in how to proceed, Ophelia was positive about one thing. She wouldn't go quietly. Nor willingly.

"There is nothing to reconsider. Even if I wasn't mated to the Glassmaker, I would ***not*** have ***you.***"

While her statement was truthful, the resulting rage displayed in Caspian's expression made her contemplate if she would've been better served by not voicing it. He'd already proven his power over their weapons. The blessed waiting for his orders could quickly overwhelm them with their numbers and various abilities. Angering him further could spell certain disaster.

"We will see about that."

Caspian's jaw was clenched as he no longer held on to his affable façade. With barely a glance to the Traveler, he tilted his head. One second, the male was standing next to Caspian, the next he was beside Ophelia's horse.

She had no opportunity to truly process what was happening. When he stretched one hand out to touch her, she acted on natural reflex and gripped his fingers. With intention, she *borrowed* his gift. Only, unlike the previous few rotations where she'd touched Magnus and Damien for a scant sand, she held on to the Traveler until he crumpled to the ground. It was necessary for her to release him then. Otherwise, his weight would've toppled her from her horse.

Sitting up straight on Starlight's back, Ophelia felt the new energy pulsing through her. They'd discussed possibilities for if they encountered trouble on their journey, but the major part of their plan included Ophelia being able to flee while the others protected her. Given the circumstances. That wasn't an option.

"EAMON!"

The way Caspian yelled his name, one would think he actually cared for the, now unconscious, Traveler. Ophelia looked to Rylan. His nod was barely perceptible, but she saw it. Allowing instinct to guide her, she located the second Traveler in Caspian's group.

With another quick prayer to the goddess, she focused on the wispy female standing to the other side of Caspian. In the space of a breath, she was no longer seated on her horse, but on the back of the second Traveler, surprising them both.

"Phely!!"

Damien's voice rang out across the expanse, but Ophelia ignored it. She knew Rylan would keep her brother from jumping into the fray to save her.

The female struggled under Ophelia's heavier frame and went to her knees. Maintaining her hold on the Traveler's shoulders, Ophelia looked back to where the other lay. In an instant they were next to the sleeping teleporter. The additional energy pumped through Ophelia's system making her feel as if she could take to flight with a simple thought. She didn't know if it were merely these Travelers or her lack of experience with the blessing, but she recognized she could only teleport to a place she could see.

"What in the goddess's name?!" Magnus exclaimed in a hushed tone.

With a shake of her head, as she stood to her feet, Ophelia cut him off.

"Prepare to fight."

Removing the Travelers from the equation helped, but they were still woefully out numbered. And, with Caspian being a Ferrokin, he'd made certain they couldn't use their weapons. He'd likely turn their own swords on them. Still, the odds didn't matter. Knowing she had limited time to use the Travelers' blessings as her own, and her lack of experience with teleporting, Ophelia relied on the guidance she was certain came straight from the goddess herself.

Caspian lifted one arm, and the contingent advanced—closing the distance between them. Without thinking about it too hard, Ophelia leapt into the air and landed on the back of the closest Brawn, giving him the same treatment she'd given the Travelers. The large male lumbered two steps more before collapsing to his knees.

The field exploded in a cacophony of sounds, and the newly acquired temporary blessings made Ophelia feel as if every nerve in her body was standing on end.

"What are you doing? Contain her!"

Caspian's directive sounded above the rest of the noise. As quickly as she could move from one being to the next, Ophelia was aware the odds still weren't in their favor. The screeching cry of the falcon above them drew her gaze to Rylan.

The only one of them possessing a weapon not made of metal, he relinquished his sword to Damien while he swung his axe. However, as strong as he was, even he wouldn't be a match for a Brawn. She was trying to determine where to go next just as a strong pair of arms wrapped around her.

The way she was grabbed, kept her from immediately laying her hands on the male lifting her from her most recent victim. It took her a second to recall her borrowed blessing. However, once she did, her assailant became a fresh contributor to her energy collection. Standing to her full height, she turned to face her next opponent.

In a semi-circle around her were a Brawn, a Seeker, and a Changer in their bear form. Neither approached, likely now understanding her touch could render them unconscious. Not wanting to yield the advantage, Ophelia didn't look to see how her mate, brother, and cousin were faring. Instead, she ensured the trio and Caspian remained in her line of sight.

A moment of despondency began to settle over her. If she didn't do something, they would be over run. She'd be forced to surrender to Caspian. And that couldn't happen. There had to be a way. Using the gifts of the Travelers and the Brawn would only take her so far.

What good was being an Ergokin and having the ability to control the energy around her, if she couldn't save herself and her loved ones? The power she'd *borrowed* pulsed around her making her skin feel charged. She flexed her fingers in an effort to maintain control. As she did so, a memory resurfaced.

The first time she'd knowingly used her blessing, she'd felt drained afterwards. She'd depleted her energy stores too quickly, giving them to Ramo. All blessings were a form of energy in practice. Ophelia had learned what made the Ergokin so special was their ability to utilize and manipulate energy.

Energy could never be destroyed, only transformed. She had no desire to amplify the blessings of Caspian's mercenaries, but she did want to level the field as much as possible.

DARIE MCCOY

Without their superior strength, and shifting abilities, the majority of his band would be useless—unlike Rylan, Damien, and Magnus who were skilled fighters without augmentation.

Once again relying on natural instinct, Ophelia lifted both arms until they were shoulder height with her palms facing outwards. Prayers to the goddess were mumbled beneath her breath as she observed the auras emanating from the beings standing before her. Curling her digits toward her palm, she envisioned herself calling the radiant colors to her fingertips.

Chapter Twenty-Seven

Rylan's heartbeat thundered in his ears. He'd had an idea of what could occur when he'd looked into Ophelia's golden eyes and nodded his understanding. He was aware he essentially gave his permission for her to put herself in harm's way. However, he also knew, without the use of Ophelia's blessing, they wouldn't end the rotation on this side of the cursed river.

They were out of options. As untried as her blessing was, she had to use it. The moment she disappeared into thin air, Rylan grabbed Starlight's reins as he called out to Damien to stop him from chasing after his sister. Not going after her himself was one of the most difficult things Rylan had ever done.

He could tell Damien was set to ignore him. But, mere sands later, Ophelia returned—only on solid ground instead of Starlight's back. She was there for a mere two blinks before she disappeared again. By then, Caspian had dispatched his troops to attack them.

Their foes had only made it a few steps when Ophelia reappeared on the back of one of the Brawns charging toward them. Releasing Starlight, Rylan tapped the mount to get her out of harm's way. She wouldn't go far. Even if she did, Damien would find her. Rylan's confidence that they'd escape this encounter with their lives, despite the overwhelming odds, could only be attributed to his faith in his Sweeting.

Her advancements with her blessing over a short duration assured him they'd only scratched the surface of her true power. A being with such potential combined with such strength of character, would not be bested by the likes of Caspian Ironshade.

Rylan didn't have much time with his thoughts as the group split with part of them attempting to corner Ophelia and the rest advancing on him, Damien, and Magnus. Caspian had rendered Damien's and Magnus' swords unusable. The Earther had resorted to commanding his use over the very soil and stones to defend them—sending the objects flying toward their attackers. Rylan removed his specially crafted glass hewn sword from his harness and tossed it to Damien as the Seeker was now without a weapon.

Guiding Shadowfox's movements using his legs, Rylan went into the fray uncaring of the odds given the blessings of those attacking them. Using the elevation of being on his mount to his advantage he swung his axe with precision, cutting down the first being he encountered. His own war cry was joined by Damien's and Magnus' as the three of them fought valiantly.

The hairs on Rylan's arms stood on end and an unexpected fission of...something... ghosted across his skin. Immediately he located Ophelia on the field. She was semi-surrounded but her foes were standing just beyond arm's reach. Only Rylan's own blessing allowed him to see what occurred next.

The reds, oranges, and golden browns associated with

Brawns, Seekers and Changers appeared to be draining away from the beings facing off against his mate. Was it possible she was transferring their blessings to herself? The movements of her hands resembled a beckoning motion, but he knew she wouldn't be inviting the three of them closer.

Rylan's suspicions were confirmed when the large brown bear reverted to a much smaller male. Looking down at himself, he released a shocked cry filled with such agony and disbelief, it drew the attention of the others. Seizing the opportunity, Rylan galloped closer to the grouping, kicking the thick-necked Brawn aside as he grasped Ophelia swinging her up behind him on his mount.

"Well done, Sweeting." He praised as he guided Shadowfox to circle back around those remaining.

Magnus had garnered the attention of the last Brawn and the Falcon overhead was attacking, causing him to split his attention as he worked to remain out of reach of the powerful Brawn while launching hardened pieces of earth at both the brutish being and the sharp taloned bird. Damien was holding his own against the Seeker, but another was working their way behind him.

"Sweeting, you help Magnus and Damien. I will deal with Caspian."

"But, Rylan—"

"No, Sweeting. They need you more than I at this moment. I have no metal in my weapons for him to control."

Not giving her a chance to protest further, he launched himself from the horse's back running full tilt toward the now retreating Caspian. True to the male Rylan deduced him to be, the moment the fight ceased to be overwhelmingly in his favor, Caspian attempted to abscond.

As he'd arrived carried by a Traveler, he had no horse to spirit him away. He was forced to use his own underused limbs to do the job. He was close to a line of trees when Rylan called out to him.

"Where do you think you're going, Caspian?" Rylan's voice boomed, filled with his anger and disdain.

"Do you think you can slink away after threatening my mate? Attempting to add her to your collection as if she was not a being with her own free will? As if she did not belong to another?"

Rylan caught up with Caspian using the blunt end of his axe to send the other male stumbling into the knee-high grass. Rylan slowed his pace to what could've been called a leisurely stroll, while Caspian scrambled trying to regain his footing.

Once he was standing, he stood to his full height tugging at the ends of his ornate outer garments to straighten them.

"Think carefully about what you are doing, Glassmaker. You may have lauded status, but I have power. Immense power."

Nodding thoughtfully, Rylan flipped the axe in his hand. He saw Caspian's focus on the blade, and suspected the other male wondered why he was unable to manipulate the weapon as he had the others. His thoughts were confirmed when Caspian flexed his fingers then formed fists at his side. The grayish aura surrounding him deepened, but his efforts were in vain. Holding the axe up for his inspection, Rylan allowed the light to reflect off the vibrant blue tones growing brighter from the head down to the blade.

"If you're expending energy attempting to control this, you're wasting it. Thunderstrike...That is its name. Is made entirely of glass. The only exception being the leather on the grip. So...no metal."

Rylan shrugged negligently as he watched Caspian go through the stages of reasoning. His eyes went to the other male's footing as Caspian took a halting step back.

"Do you really believe running away is still an option, Caspian?"

Puffing out his chest. Caspian drew himself up as if he hadn't just contemplated making a mad dash.

"Run? Run from who? You, Glassmaker? Why would I run from you? It is you who should run. Away from your so-called mate.

You also owe me thanks. I was trying to do what was best for the realm. No one being should possess the power given to the Ergokin. Do you realize she could control us all at her whim? ***All of us!*** A creature like that must be contained."

Flames ignited beneath Rylan's skin. "Creature? Did you just form your mouth to call my mate a creature?"

Placing his hands up between them, Caspian attempted to side step away.

"You know what I am saying, Glassmaker. You would kill me for telling the truth? Ergokin are unnatural. Why do you think there is no one in living memory who has met one?"

Rylan had many questions to point out Caspian's hypocrisy. There were countless things he could say to dispute what the other male said. But Rylan was a being of few words allowing his actions to speak for him. Before Caspian was aware of his circumstances, Rylan flicked his wrist. A shocked expression was frozen on Caspian's face as his head toppled from his body.

He would have no further opportunity for a long villainous speech with which to spew his envy and hatred. In essence, it is what it boiled down to. His envy, of Ophelia's blessing and the blessings of others more powerful than him, drove him to collect them. To control them. His reign ended this rotation. Caspian of the Ironshades would no longer be a scourge on the realm.

Turning away from the two pieces of Caspian in the grass, Rylan sought his mate and the others across the clearing. It was the other reason he couldn't indulge Caspian in his fruit-less efforts. Rylan needed to get back to his mate.

What he saw when he located their group made him take off in a dead run trying to reach his Sweeting. His heart leapt into his throat as his long legs ate up the distance separating them.

Chapter Twenty-Eight

Ophelia sat atop Rylan's huge mount watching him race away after Caspian. Her confidence in him didn't prevent her from being concerned. Rylan's blessing wasn't one which could be used defensively, while Caspian seemed to have done nothing aside from learning how to weaponize his.

Grunts and shouts drew her attention back to her brother and the beings he and Magnus were battling. They'd both left their mounts and were on foot. This rotation the goddess would tire of hearing Ophelia's voice, because she mumbled another prayer as she goaded Shadowfox into a trot. Buoyed by her recent success, she performed the same motion she'd used on her most recent foes.

When the falcon released a shriek which transformed into a yelp as the male plummeted to the ground, Magnus released a corresponding yell. Charging the Brawn who'd been attacking him, he slung a volley of stone and hardened earth at the large male, soon overwhelming him.

Ophelia wasn't certain how much help it would be to Damien to temporarily relieve the Seekers he fought of their blessing. So, she appeared behind one of them, placing her hand on his neck. Beneath her firm grasp, he lost consciousness rather quickly. Now faced with reduced numbers, the remaining Seeker opted to run away.

Cutting a zig zagging path through his fallen comrades, he ran without once stopping to see if any of them were alive or conscious. The tacit agreement among them, to simply allow him to flee, was unspoken. The first teleporter moaned on the ground and Ophelia contemplated touching him again, but her attention was redirected by Damien's tap on her shoulder.

"Phely, look."

An ornate carriage approached flanked, by large males in battle gear. Riding in an uncovered wagon, were three of the males who'd previously accompanied Caspian. They were the Changer, Seeker and Brawn who'd fled when Rylan trampled through their attack on Ophelia. The Seeker who'd just run away, was quickly added to the collection. There was no crest on the carriage nor did the shiny obsidian armor worn by the contingent bear any clear markings.

Gathering at her sides, Magnus and Damien readied their swords. The urge rose in Ophelia to seek out Rylan, but she didn't know the purpose of these new players. If they were unfriendly, she didn't want to alert them to his presence.

The carriage rolled to a stop and the armored males fanned out into an impressive line before them. Without a word, the driver of the carriage stepped down from his perch. Opening the door, he extended his arm inside the darkened interior. When he drew back, a single gloved hand was in his.

Soon, a beautiful female appeared. The simple appearance of her clothing belied the ornateness of the transport. However, closer inspection of the garments revealed they were of excellent quality.

"Calm, everyone. No one is going to harm you."

Raising her hands, she motioned for them to lower their

weapons. Ophelia wasn't surprised when Damien and Magnus immediately complied.

The unknown female's voice was a pleasant timbre. The warmth in her tone made Ophelia feel as if she was a youngling again being wrapped in her mama's embrace. Her rich, dark skin held a timeless quality making it impossible to determine her age. She could match Ophelia's thirty-four winters or triple them. No one would know from her outward appearance.

The driver accompanied her as she stepped closer to them. Radiance created a full body halo around her in colors Ophelia couldn't begin to describe. Parts of it were so bright they were nearly blinding. Yet a darkness moved within the brightness which was so devoid of color, it was like peering into the abyss.

Her armored entourage moved with her, until she instructed them to stop with a slight wave of one hand.

"I am the Keeper of the Blessings." She looked at the three of them, pausing to make eye contact with each, starting with the males.

"Welcome, Seeker, Damien, eldest son of the Leander Patriarch Theron and mate to Selene. Earther, Magnus, third son of the second son in the Blackwood line, and mate to Valeria."

She stared at Ophelia with a soft smile on her face. "And you. Welcome, Ergokin, Ophelia, only daughter of the Leander, mate to the Glassmaker Rylan of the Sunweavers heir of the Firefists."

Ophelia's sharp inhale was drowned out by the clanking of metal as the soldiers reformed in a circle facing outward. Following the direction of their stance, she saw Rylan approaching at breakneck speed. His axe gleamed in his hand; the sunlight reflected off the shades of blue in a dazzling effect. Long dark brown hair was whipped back by the wind away from his face etched with concern.

Without regard to the armed males, Ophelia broke away from the group to meet him. Peripherally, she heard the Keeper instruct her guards to stand down. However, Ophelia didn't look back. She didn't stop until she was in Rylan's embrace. He held her close with bone-cracking firmness. She allowed him as much time as he needed to hold her patting her body, assuring himself she was okay.

She allowed it because she needed the same. Her heart lifted at seeing him whole and unharmed. Aside from the loss of the binder taming his hair, he physically appeared the same as when they'd broken camp that morning.

"Are you okay, Sweeting? Why are there more warriors? Who are they?"

Cupping his face in her hands, Ophelia captured his eyes. "I am well, Glassmaker. Come. Meet the Keeper of the Blessings."

"The Keeper?" Rylan looked over her shoulder.

He didn't object when she stepped out of his arms, clasping one of his hands in hers. They approached the silent group together. The last part of what the Keeper had said to her was burning Ophelia's brain. She hadn't mentioned it to Rylan because she was still trying to process what it meant.

Once they came to a stop next to Damien, the Keeper turned her gaze onto Rylan.

"Greetings, Glassmaker, Rylan, only son of Atticus of the Sunweavers, mate to Ophelia and the heir of the Firefists."

Rylan's fingers clenched around Ophelia's prompting her to pat the top of his hand soothingly as she peered up at him. His erect posture was stiffer than hardened steel as he stared unblinkingly at the Keeper. In turn, she smiled and inclined her head.

"Come. We have much to discuss." Looking at her protectors, she gestured to the reawakening band of the blessed littering the field. "Put them in the wagon. They will require attention."

When Ophelia, Rylan and the others remained rooted in their spot, the Keeper made a shooing motion.

"If you wish to know more, get your horses and come with us."

The words had the desired effect. Damien whistled for his horse, and Blaze came thundering across the field with Starlight and Spirit trailing behind him. Shadowfox hadn't strayed as far, so a click from Rylan had the horse at his side.

As they remounted and waited for the rest of Caspian's contingent to be secured in the uncovered wagon, Rylan and Ophelia shared questioning looks between them. They both wanted answers to what the Keeper proclaimed when she'd met them. He was the heir of the Firefists? The family at the root of the Leander family shame? How was it possible?

The only way to find out was to do as the Keeper instructed—follow her. So, that is what they did.

Chapter Twenty-Nine

Rylan's thoughts churned as they traveled the well-worn road toward Ashenford, the village closest to the Keeper's estate. Much like the Leander's, her estate resembled a castle, complete with stone walls and an outer ring of smaller thatched roof homes. Traveling via the known path cut the length of the journey considerably.

The sun had just reached its midday peak when they entered the gates. Sweeping his gaze over their surroundings, Rylan noted very few of the small abodes were unoccupied. Beings stood either outside or directly in the doorway calling out greetings to the Keeper as the carriage passed. They appeared genuinely happy to see her.

Instead of riding inside the carriage, she sat beside the driver waving and responding to each by name. Although he could see the curiosity in the stares of those who watched them, none of them voiced it. They simply watched and murmured amongst themselves.

It wasn't difficult to relate to their unabashed interest. His desire for answers had set his thoughts ablaze. It was well known the Keeper possessed the knowledge gained through the Chroniclers of the blessings read by all in the realm. However, he'd never been informed of the things she revealed to him in her greeting.

The Sunweavers had a large number of Glassmakers in their line. It was almost seen as the goddess had deemed their line created for the purpose of proclaiming blessings. It wasn't until he'd traveled to Misthaven that he'd ever heard of the Firefist line. How could he possibly be the heir?

They were led into the inner ring of the castle wall. More males, dressed similarly to the guards escorting them, were just inside. While they were equipped with weapons, they weren't clothed in the same degree of armor as the others. *Why did the Keeper need such protection?*

Rylan had been told by his elders gaining an audience with the Keeper was difficult. However, since he'd never been in her presence before, he had no understanding of the degree to which she was insulated from those outside her protective walls.

Stable boys met them to take their horses and care for them. Those who'd accompanied Caspian in his attempt to abduct Ophelia were taken in the opposite direction as Rylan and the others were escorted into the great hall of the dwelling. He observed them being driven away as he noted their condition. Some still appeared dazed and hadn't regained their colorful auras denoting their gift.

"This way." The Keeper's pleasing voice instructed them as she held out her arm indicating the area away from the hearth.

A large cookpot hung over a low flame. Light steam and a savory aroma issued from the contents within. Rylan found it curious, since a keep this size typically had an attached kitchen or one nearby.

She stopped before an assembly of furnishings, taking a seat in a plush stuffed chair. A tufted stool was placed nearby.

When an attendant moved to place it beneath her feet, she waved them away.

"Please. Sit." The Keeper's outstretched arm indicated similarly appointed divans and chairs.

Rylan wasn't certain what he expected, but it wasn't the warmth and feeling of home he experienced within the Keeper's walls. With Ophelia's hand clasped in his, he guided her to the divan. Sitting after she'd selected her place, he returned his gaze to the female who was the realm's repository of knowledge regarding the blessed.

"I know you have many questions. And I will answer them. The mid rotation meal is being held for us. Would you care to partake now or wait? The choice is yours."

It may have been selfish, but Rylan didn't want to wait. Still, he looked at his Sweeting to gauge her feelings before responding. She gripped his hand in their silent conversation, giving a nod of ascent. Damien and Magnus settled their backs into their respective seats as if it was a foregone conclusion they would wait for the meal.

"We will wait." To his own ears, Rylan's voice sounded rough. As though the sand which formed his glass had scraped his vocal cords.

"I thought so." The Keeper's smile brightened her already beautiful visage. There was something familiar in it, but Rylan couldn't name it.

"At least have something to quench your thirst as we talk."

At the mention of libations, household staff appeared bearing trays containing drinking vessels. His first sip of the beverage was quickly followed by a deep gulp as he slaked the thirst he hadn't been aware existed.

When he finished, he noticed the satisfied expression on the Keeper's face as she regarded them. Warmth emanated from her as much as the multicolored aura surrounding her body did. From the table next to her, she produced a large leather-bound book. Placing it on her lap, she flipped it open without bothering to look down at the pages.

"You have waited patiently for the answers you seek. However, I have one query before I give them. I'm aware you were on your way to me when I encountered you on the road. There are many in the realm who make certain to tell me of such things.

When there seemed to be a delay in your appearance, I thought it best to ride out and investigate for myself. Glassmaker, you have served diligently for many winters. There has never been a time when you weren't available to update the Chronicler on the blessings you'd proclaimed.

That is until you read the sparks for your mate. The first Ergokin born in the realm in untold ages. Why would you not continue in your duty as usual? Why did you abandon your post in Thistledown?"

Although her question could be taken as an accusation, it didn't feel as such to Rylan. It felt more like an opportunity to reveal than explain. Looking at his mate, he detected the acceptance and encouragement in her expression.

"Keeper, you are aware of all blessings proclaimed in the realm. So, you know of Caspian Ironshade."

"Yes."

"Were you aware of the large number of blessed housed in his vast holdings near Thistledown?"

"I am made aware of the blessings, names of those associated and their lineage. I know Thistledown and the lands surrounding have a large number of blessed living there."

"Yes, there are a large number of blessed. I suspected Caspian was involved in unscrupulous dealings. He proclaimed he was a benefactor to the many blessed who lived on his lands. But I never trusted it was anything so altruistic.

The rotation I read the sparks for Ophelia was the same rotation he came to have them read for a young Hydrokin. I couldn't be certain, but I sensed danger in his knowledge of her blessing. He was a male who believed himself above others, and that nothing he desired should be denied to him. I feared for her safety.

As you said, there hasn't been an Ergokin born in many generations. I know of no one with living memory of encountering one with such a blessing. So, instead of allowing her and her brothers to leave alone while I waited to update the Chronicler, I left with them. It was my belief that the fewer people who knew of the reading, the safer she would be."

Nodding in understanding, the Keeper splayed her fingers flat over the pages.

"Is concern the reason you mated with her?"

"No!"

Rylan sat up straighter with his emphatic denial. His eyes immediately sought his Sweeting's golden pools. Air eased from his lungs as he saw the depth of caring reflected back at him. She didn't believe he'd mated her simply to keep her safe. It was all that mattered to him. When he looked back at the Keeper, she wore another blindingly bright smile.

"That's good. I wasn't sure if the Leander Soulkin had made you aware of the mating thread binding the two of you together."

Ophelia's breath hitched at her mention of Kieran, and Rylan squeezed her fingers lending her his support, as she'd done for him. Dipping his chin in acknowledgement, he held the Keeper's gaze.

"He did, but I'd already determined she was my mate before he confirmed the bond."

If it were possible, her smile brightened even further.

"That is as it should be. Now, I know you have questions for me. Ask."

Rylan needed no further invitation. Clearing his throat, he asked the most immediate question on his mind.

"When you greeted me earlier, you called me the heir of the Firefists. Why? I've heard stories of my lineage from my parents and elders. None of them have ever mentioned ties to the Firefists."

The Keeper's demeanor took on a tinge of sadness. Tapping the open pages of the book, she turned it around to face him and lifted it so they all could see the image and neat letters scrawled on the linen paper.

Chapter Thirty

Ophelia couldn't define the emotions she felt wafting from Rylan as they all stared at the open book the Keeper presented to them. At first glance, it appeared to be something of a family tree, but at one point, some generations back, the many branches became one. One son to carry on the Firefist line. Since it was patriarchal, it would seem to end at that last male.

However, there were additional names, females listed as branches shooting off the final male. Under those names were names of other females until...near the bottom right of the second page, there was a male. Rylan born of Atticus Sunweaver and Calliope Earthsong. His mother was listed as the sole survivor of the Firefist line.

All this time, the Leanders thought their ostracization was due to the broken oath with the Firefists, while the Firefist name had literally died out one generation following the war with their family. It is no wonder the Leanders were seen as villains. They were viewed as the family who was willing to destroy another in the name of love.

If she hadn't already been seated, Ophelia had no doubt her legs would've refused to support her weight. It took a moment for her to gather herself enough to look at Rylan. His gaze remained riveted to the page. When he spoke, his gruff voice was barely above a whisper.

"My mother never told me."

"It is likely she didn't know herself." The Keeper's fingertips pressed lightly against the page as she spoke. "If they hadn't each been given a blessing from the goddess, it could've fallen from memory altogether. Similar to the history of the Ergokin."

Sensing her mate's need for support, Ophelia pressed her other hand to the back of the one he held hers in. Rubbing in soothing circles, she tried to lend him strength and peace.

"The conflict between the Firefists and the Leanders devastated both families in different ways. But now, through the two of you, the original mating oath can be honored, bringing an end to the strife on both sides."

All eyes turned to Damien when he spoke up. "How can you say such a thing Keeper? The Firefists may have an heir, but he doesn't carry the family name."

Pinning him with a shrewd look, she lifted her brows in question. "Are you not aware, youngling, that the true blood of all beings flows from the *mother*, not the *father*? If we were to truly reflect that, we'd have to claim both our maternal and paternal heritage. And in this household, we do."

Damien looked properly chastised. Wisely, he clamped his lips shut and sat back in his chair. As he did so, footsteps echoed loudly against the stone floors.

"There you are, my heart!" A large male with a shock of auburn hair strode into the room. When he reached the Keeper, he leaned over placing a kiss on her upturned lips.

"I see you located our guests."

"I did, my heart." She cupped the side of his bearded face matching the smile he wore. When he stood straight beside her, they tangled their fingers together resting them on her shoulder.

"Finnian, my heart, meet Damien, Magnus, Ophelia and Rylan. Everyone, meet my life mate Finnian."

The love between the two was apparent. They were both radiant with the strength of their bond. Ophelia wondered if she and Rylan's bond would ever be so noticeable as theirs. Finnian tilted his head in greeting. When the Keeper released his hand, he remained standing at her side with one hand on her shoulder.

"Now. Where was I? Oh! Yes, I remember. The mating between Ophelia and Rylan satisfies the terms of the mating oath, but it does so much more."

Ophelia sat up straighter gripping Rylan's fingers when the Keeper's gaze landed on them once again. Tingles began at the base of her spine and spread like tiny butterfly wings beating against her skin.

"Your ancestor was given a prophesy from the Enchantress. Do you remember it?"

"Yes." Ophelia nodded. "*One will come, and she will wield magicks which haven't been seen in this realm for generations. She will be born to the blood of Leander. Through her, the line will be restored.*"

The Keeper's chin dipped as she listened. However, a frown marred her unblemished face when Ophelia stopped speaking. Ophelia couldn't stop herself from asking, "did I say it wrong?"

"No, youngling. You didn't say it wrong. Is that all you remember?"

Ophelia's eyes widened at the implication there was more than what she was told.

"Yes. I recited it word for word as told to me by my papa, who was told by his papa."

The Keeper flipped to a different page in her book, making a tsking sound as she did so.

"It would seem that your papa and his papa didn't recall the entire prophesy."

"You mean there was more?"

"Of course. There's always more."

Everyone, except Finnian leaned forward attentively. The anticipation of her next words was its own entity hanging over the space. When the Keeper next spoke, they listened without even the sound of their breathing to obscure her words.

"The rest of the prophesy is... *She will be one who seeks to make this realm better in all ways, a helper who shines her bright light on those around her, lifting them higher. Her lot will not be solely to restore honor to her family, but she will be a being capable of wielding all the blessings and the keeper thereof.*"

Ophelia was frozen in time. The breath she held remained trapped in her lungs as she stared without seeing. She wanted to question the truth of the words spoken, but the Keeper had read them directly from the pages of the Ledger, the book of blessings. *How had her family lost such a monumental part of the prophecy? What did this mean?*

Damien, forever the big brother, broke the heavy silence. "Keeper, are you saying my sister is destined to become the new Keeper?"

"Yes." The Keeper's answer was given without guile nor further explanation.

The warmth and weight of Rylan's arm enclosed around Ophelia's shoulders. "Breathe, Sweeting."

Until he said the words, the air was imprisoned inside her stunned body. With them, she released it in a whoosh. Leaning into Rylan, she accepted his physical support. The Keeper regarded her with kind eyes.

"I know this comes as a shock. When I learned you were

traveling here, I thought you knew the whole of things—especially given the name your parents bestowed upon you."

Ophelia lifted slightly within Rylan's hold. "What about my name?"

"Why, the very origin of the name Ophelia, is help. Giving you such a name was itself a proclamation. You are a helper in name and deed."

Ophelia couldn't argue the assessment. She'd prided herself in aiding her family with whatever skills she possessed in the absence of a blessing from the goddess. Never did she think she was living the prophesy as it was foretold even then.

"Your mating with the Glassmaker completes the circle, and lets me know that you truly are the one for whom we've waited."

"We?" Ophelia latched onto the single word.

"Yes. We. Finnian and I have served the realm for more than two millennia. It is time for the next Keeper and *her* Glassmaker to take on the role."

The emphasis, the Keeper placed on 'her' drew Ophelia's gaze to the male standing beside her. Truly looking at him beyond his shock of auburn hair, Ophelia noted he was dressed in a manner similar to Rylan's attire when she'd first met him in his workshop. The Keeper's mate was a Glassmaker. Ophelia's jaw dropped, her mouth hanging open as she attempted to integrate the mountain of information she'd been given.

Nodding in understanding, the Keeper stood. Finnian immediately took her hand in his and the two looked at the rest of them.

"I gave you the option of waiting, but maybe these revelations would be easier to digest over a meal. Come. Let's break our fast."

Ignoring her brother's probing stare, Ophelia accepted Rylan's assistance in standing. They followed the couple to the long table set up near the hearth. Soon, the savory contents of the large cookpot were revealed when they were served a hearty stew. At her first deep inhale, Ophelia conceded the Keeper's point. Nourishment was definitely required to help navigate this new development.

Over a sumptuous fare, the Keeper explained how the Ergokin was always the next Keeper. She, herself, was nearly as many winters old as Ophelia when she met Finnian and he read the sparks for her. Unlike Ophelia, the Keeper's family hadn't been given a prophecy from the Enchantress. So, when no obvious blessing manifested, she was considered unblessed.

Once Finnian declared her blessing, and they were mated, they hadn't sought out the Keeper as Rylan suggested to Ophelia. The Keeper found them.

"The former Keeper, Lyra, found us living outside the village Finnian settled in once he'd completed his apprenticeship. At that time, I'd only scratched the surface of what an Ergokin could do."

Ophelia leaned forward, enthralled as the Keeper revealed more. "It was her who told me why Finnian was able to discern my blessing before he ever read the sparks—why he was the only Glassmaker powerful enough to read the sparks of an Ergokin."

Although she wanted to know more of what the Keeper alluded to regarding Rylan, another question burned in Ophelia's mind.

"If you're Ergokin, like me. Why are the colors surrounding you so different?"

Placing her utensils next to her plate, the Keeper folded her hands in her lap.

"That's a very good question. Over time, as an Ergokin's strength grows, her aura changes to reflect the amalgamation of blessings residing in her being. At present, it seems you can only amplify, mute or *borrow* another's blessing.

One day, once you've fully mastered your blessing, you'll be able to do more than temporarily use those blessings. They will remain within you, as they do within me. That you see the colors at all is a testament to the strength of your blessing."

Ophelia's head spun from yet another revelation. Stealing a glance at Rylan, she met his gaze. His expression was filled with equal parts admiration and pride. The warmth of his hand comforted her has he squeezed her leg in assurance, keeping her present in the moment.

Chapter Thirty-One

That night, as they lie beneath the plush bedding in the chambers they were given, Rylan held Ophelia in his arms thinking. Not simply about the events of the rotation, but the handful of rotations before and after his Sweeting stepped into his workshop and altered his world. Over their meal and for hours after, the Keeper enlightened them regarding the true role of an Ergokin within the realm.

As with many things, much is lost to memory the more time passes. They become myth and legend. Just as it happened with the prophesy from the Enchantress, it happened with the relationship between the Keeper of the blessings and the Ergokin. There was only one Ergokin born every third millennia.

Learning the true mate of every Ergokin was a Glassmaker, was eye opening for Rylan. He'd had no idea only her true mate's gift would be strong enough to allow him to read her blessing in the sparks. All other's would be overcome by the sheer strength of her power. Rylan had also learned his gift was amplified simply being in Ophelia's presence and grew once they were fully mated.

Ophelia shifted against his side, releasing a puff of air into his neck. Squeezing her gently, he rubbed her hip.

"Are you well, Sweeting?"

"I suppose." Walking her fingers up his chest, she captured a few strands of his beard, tugging gently. "My head is overflowing with everything that Aurora spoke of."

The Keeper had insisted they call her by her given name. She thought it made more sense seeing as Ophelia was also the Keeper. Thankfully, she wasn't expected to start immediately, but they would both have to spend time with Aurora and Finnian learning their new roles.

"It's understandable. It isn't every rotation one learns they are to be the repository of knowledge for an entire realm. You'll require at least fifteen sands to get used to the idea."

Ophelia's light giggles were accompanied by a harmless tug on his beard.

"Fifteen whole sands? That's exceedingly generous of you, Glassmaker."

"I'm a generous being, Sweeting."

The breath Rylan released was so close to a sigh, he startled himself. He wasn't a male given to sighing. However, before he'd mated with Ophelia, he also wasn't given to wearing silly, lovesick smiles. Yet, here he lay, grinning like a loon because his mate was in his arms pulling on his beard.

"Rylan?"

"Yes, Sweeting."

"What happened with Caspian?"

They hadn't spoken of Caspian since Rylan leapt off his horse in pursuit of him. There hadn't been a time when they were alone. And, the appearance of the Keeper drew their attention for a considerable amount of it. Holding her within his embrace, he didn't want to dwell on the ugliness that brought them to this point. However, he'd learned his Sweeting wouldn't be easily deterred.

In his normal succinct fashion, Rylan responded.

"We fought. He lost."

A grumble rumbled in his chest when Ophelia sat up, pulling her softness away from his side.

"That's all? You fought. He lost?"

"What else would you like for me to say, Sweeting? I won't describe how he lost. You only need concern yourself with the knowledge he will no longer be able to bring harm to another soul."

The way she pursed her lips made him desire to kiss them, but her stiff arm against his chest prevented it.

"Speaking of souls, what do you think of what Finnian and Aurora suggested regarding those under Caspian's control?"

"It's difficult for me to understand their willingness to attempt to force you into a life you didn't want, simply because he told them he desired you. There were no younglings in the group he brought with him. More than half had blessings which would allow them to overpower him at any moment."

"So, you believe giving them the opportunity to start new lives is too lenient?"

Cupping the side of her face, Rylan stared into her eyes. "Sweeting, I will always believe anyone willing to purposely do you harm shouldn't be allowed to continue existing. So, yes. Freedom is too lenient."

Ophelia leaned closer. Not as close as Rylan desired, but closer. "Glassmaker, neither of us know the true depth of the hold Caspian had on them, nor for how long. Remember the youngling he brought to you? The Hydrokin? He was no more than eight winters.

If a being has been controlled from such a young age, they don't always recognize the ways they can free themselves. It's similar to how the Leanders have been thriving for some time, but didn't believe in their redemption until my blessing was declared. I did nothing different, but they wouldn't believe in an end to our family shame until the sparks declared me to be the one spoken of by the Enchantress."

Tangling his fingers in the hair at her nape, Rylan tugged her closer. Lifting from the pillow, he placed a kiss on her soft lips.

"One of the many things I love about you, Sweeting, is your ability to see things I am unable to discern."

Ophelia gasped. Soft fingers ghosted across his lips. He kissed them before capturing her hand in his.

"You love me, Glassmaker?"

"Of course I do, Sweeting."

Sitting up fully, Rylan arranged her straddling his lap. When they were eye to eye, he cradled her head in his hands.

"Did you not know? I have loved you from the moment you entered my workshop. From then on, my feelings for you have only grown."

Kissing the tip of her nose, then her eyelids, Rylan pulled back slightly, piercing her with his gaze.

"My heart soared when the Keeper said we'd always been destined for one another. I've never felt so complete and full of purpose as I have from the instant I saw your beautiful face."

Swiping at the tears streaking Ophelia's cheeks, Rylan wondered if he'd said the wrong thing.

Obviously sensing his concern, his mate placed her hands on his beard, stroking him. "I am well, Glassmaker. I'm simply overjoyed. I love you more than I ever imagined loving another being. Hearing you feel the same fills my heart to bursting."

Relief flooded his senses. Taking her lips in another kiss, he tried to convey the depth of his feelings with his touch. Her admission of love affected him in more ways than one. His desire to physically join them together as a testament ramped up.

When Ophelia rotated her hips gliding her feminine folds against him, he was emboldened. She wanted him in the same way. Grasping her plush bottom in his hands, he guided her movements.

Rylan inhaled Ophelia's exhale as he empaled her on his turgid length. Swallowing her moans, he steered her in her riding. Adding his own groans of appreciation, he poured all of his adoration into the moment. Seeing a glimpse of their future, knowing he had more than a millennia ahead of him to love Ophelia was an indescribable feeling.

Tearing her lips from his, Ophelia tossed her head back as her movements increased. Her silken walls clamped around him enticing his seed from his sacs.

"That's it, Sweeting. Give it all to your Glassmaker."

Gritting his teeth, Rylan held onto her, allowing her to set the pace. She was so beautiful in her pleasure, simply observing her was enough to send him over the edge. However, the fluttering of her heated tunnel is what finally made him grab her hips, roll her beneath him, and stroke her honied walls until they both tipped over into bliss.

As they came down from their explosive joining, Rylan caressed Ophelia's hair admiring the glow of her skin. She had the appearance of a female who'd been loved well and hard. When she lifted her eyelids, he met her languid smile with one of his own.

"I love you, Glassmaker."

"And I love you to the end of eternity, my helper."

The End

Glossary of Terms

Brawn – possesses near super human strength.

Bender – is essentially an illusionist who can bend people's perception of others and their surroundings.

Blessing—the special gift/power bestowed by the goddess.

Changer – a shape shifter primarily those who can shift into animal form. Most can only assume one form.

Chronicler – a village record keeper who records the glassmakers' proclamations of those who come before them to learn their blessing.

Diviner – Has the ability to touch objects and see flashes of a person's life or future. It isn't always 100% clear. It depends on the strength of the gift.

Earther –have a connection to the actual earth who can manipulate it to grow food, soften, harden or move it at will.

Enchantress – has the gift of precognition. She doesn't have to be in the presence of the person to see their future.

Ergokin – have the ability to influence the movement of energy, in all it's forms. They can also mute or block the energy which allows other blessed beings to use their gifts. So, they can amplify other's blessings or make them completely unusable.

Ferrokin – have the ability to control metals as well as detecting them within other objects such as deep within the earth.

Healer – has a healing touch and the ability to use herbs facilitate healing of most ailments.

Hydrokin – have the ability to control water in any form, even to the point of gathering moisture in the air to make it rain.

Glydder (glider) –A mind reader. They can read the thoughts of others be them conscious or subconscious thought.

Keeper – The record keeper of the realm. They maintain The Ledger tracking all the blessings bestowed on each person going back for generations.

Luminary – Can project light. The less powerful can light their fingertips. The more powerful can cast light from their entire body.

Millennia –More than a thousand revolutions (years)

Phytokin – can control plant life causing things to grow or bloom from withered remains. They are similar to Earthers, but they can't manipulate the soil.

Qarikin— can hide or obscure himself, others and their tracks

Rotation – Days

Revolutions – Years

Sands – passing of time. Minutes, hours.

Soulkin – Can visually see the mate bond/ties between two beings, even before they've bonded physically.

Spellcaster –Similar to a sorcerer or a witch

Vane –can predict and control weather patterns

Afterword

Inspiration can come from a million different things. Writers can walk down the street and hear a noise, see a shiny object, or stumble over nothing that seems important, and it will lead to a story. When you put multiple authors together, they feed off each other, lift each other up, and find a way to push each other when we want to walk away. Our group came together, experienced the same thing (a glass blowing class) and wrote six stories, taking them in six different directions: Mystery, Sci-Fi Romance, Middle Grade Adventure, Fantasy Romance, Women's Fiction and Paranormal Romance.

Please check out all six authors who are ready to entertain book lovers who read everything: Michel Prince, J. Jorgenson J., Michele Shriver, Lizbeth Selvig, Darie McCoy, and Tara Vasser.

Find their stories at your favorite E-tailers.

Acknowledgments

My sincere thanks to my readers. Y'all are willing to go with me wherever my imagination takes me, and I can't tell you how much it means. To the Wild Writers, finding you ladies has helped me grow so much as an author. I learn something about myself and improving my craft each time we are together. Dahlia and Michel, thank you for always answering my random questions, providing insight, and reading my rough copy when I need you. To my family who has been tremendously supportive on this writing journey, it fills my heart to bursting to know you're always behind me. To Kenya Goree-Bell and Evelyn Sola, thank you for lending me your eyes and expertise. Your feedback and encouragement was invaluable. And last, but not least, I would be remiss if I didn't thank the best writing partners a girl could ever ask for. Brianna and Niccoyan, thank you for always being my sounding board and pushing me to let my characters be great. Because of you, I'll continue to 'Write that down'!

About the Author

Darie McCoy is an independent author of contemporary, interracial, romantic suspense, and paranormal/shifter romance books. A reader first, she enjoys reading books across many genres although romance holds a special place in her heart. Her experience working in a STEM field offers her a unique perspective which she uses in each story she pens.

When she doesn't have her nose in a book or her fingers on the keyboard, Darie enjoys working in her vegetable garden. A serial hobbyist, she also enjoys knitting, sewing, baking and canning. One of her favorite treats to make is salted caramel popcorn. Amongst her friends, she's known to transport the sweet treat in large quantities to share whenever they get together.

Born and raised in the south, Darie stands by the staunchly held southern sentiments that the best tea is sweet tea and college football is life.

Also by Darie McCoy

Central Valley Pack Series

Chosen

Healed

Frost Family Series

For Real

Sano's Queen (A Novella)

Christmas Candy

Draft Pick Series

Draft Pick Season I: Carver

Draft Pick Season II: Andrei

Draft Pick Season III: Denzel (Kindle Vella)

Other books/stories

Involuntary

Just Kiss Me (Part of Cupid's Kiss Anthology)

Toad: Sin City MC Oakland

Controlled Desire: Fall of Desire

www.ingramcontent.com/pod-product-compliance
Lightning Source LLC
Chambersburg PA
CBHW061153170626
46809CB00003B/1073